PINK CLUB

By Emma Bruce

Cover by Marie-Louise O'Neill

Editing/Formatting by Melanie Lopata ~ Get It Write (www.getitwriteeditingco.com)

ISBN: 9798489850346

First Edition

Acknowledgements

Firstly, I would like to thank my parents Bruce and Sheila for doing such an amazing job bringing me up and giving me just the most amazing childhood and life anyone could ever wish for. Your encouragement with my writing has been what spurred me on over the past five years, putting this project together. Just as you are undoubtedly very proud parents to one of your awesome daughters, I, too, am very proud of you because of how lucky I am to be able to call you my mum and dad! The luckiest woman in the world that's who!

Secondly, I would like to thank my husband for watching our children giving me the time to write when needed and always giving me love and support for all my decisions when investing in necessary people along the way to bring this to fruition. Love you to the moon and back. xxx

I would also like to acknowledge some very special people who have been with me through varying degrees of this journey: Holly—who has pretty much been there since this all began in 2016: Thank you for your wisdom and bringing my attention to the power of self-publishing. The awesome author, Duncan Falconer, of books such as The Hostage & The Hijack: Thanks for introducing me to the amazing and phenomenal Barri Evins! Without her coming to my rescue and saving my bacon, I highly suspect Pink Club may have become a non-event, and that would have been a tragedy, which I'm sure you—as the readers—will agree with once you fall in love (hopefully) with the story and its characters.

To my editor, Melanie Lopata (Get It Write Editing), and my book cover designer, Marie-Louise O'Neill: Thank you so much for keeping everything running smoothly in the final stages. I have learned my lesson about the em dashes (Melanie) and will be hands-off with future manuscripts.

Thank you to my friends Alan and Marie who kept me grounded on the process and for Marie for speed reading with her super-human talent, helping me weave a better flowing story and pointing out where I can add more texture with proper factual information. (You are both my secret weapons).

~ *Chapter 1*~

My name is Darla Pebble, and I live in a small one bedroom, one bathroom apartment with my mum, Rumer Pebble and our beloved rescue cat, Binks, in a scruffier area of the city of London. Mum has the tiny closet-come-bedroom, and I sleep on the sofa bed in the tiny living area which is complete with a minuscule kitchenette.

There is no privacy apart from the bathroom, so that means an absolute no-no when it comes to dating or inviting a man over. At twenty-three years old, I simply despair at times for myself. I am single and *not* living the dream by any stretch of the imagination.

My father has never been in the picture. I am the result of a one-night stand, and by the time Mum knew she was carrying me, he had well and truly disappeared into the ether, never to resurface. The fact that Mum only loosely remembered the sound of his first name doesn't help matters, and I wouldn't have been convinced if his first name was what she said it was. What she *did* know, however, was that he had certainly been German from his accent. Not that it mattered, though, because I highly doubt anyone has found someone just by typing in a search engine "German man with a name that sounds like…"

Currently, to ensure that Mum and I have food in our tummies and a roof over our heads, I work two jobs. By day I am a waitress at a quaint little Italian bistro called Chef No. 9. It is situated in a more 'up market' area of London next to the Thames, and not terribly far from The Globe Theatre.

By night, I dance at a nightclub called Lucifer's Haven, which is at an end of the city where stags go for one last hoo-rah before the "old ball and chain" becomes a permanent fixture in their lives, or where already-married men and single guys go to forget the worries of married and troubled single life.

My mother works for a local low-budget supermarket chain, and I'm glad someone agreed to employ her after a…*turbulent* evening, where she accidentally crashed some poor sod's wedding—more on that later.

Looking out of my bedroom window this morning, I notice the weather is particularly grey and drizzly. My retro radio's alarm clock is currently blaring out a rock number. Binks shoots off the end of my bed to the safety of his little cat cave when the damn thing went off, scaring both of us half to death. I've since made a mental note to perhaps tune classical FM to my morning alarm instead of the local radio station. Binks, now puffed up, resembles something of a grey ball of fur with amber eyes, still glaring at me with disdain. I ponder sometimes at what the little guy might say to me if he could talk, but his eyes communicate enough, allowing me to know he's more than just a little perturbed.

"Sorry, buddy!" I exclaim as I sleepily stretch, yawn and roll out of the sofa bed.

My feet are aching from recent rehearsed dance routines. The cold and damp weather doesn't help either, as it always seems to make the pain worse. On my weekends off, I attend a local street dance class which is run by my friend and dance teacher, Dante Collins. His classes help me pick up inspiration for my dancing routines at Lucifer's Haven. The more inventive I can be, the bigger tips I make. Although, in reality, there isn't much a podium dancer can do to draw drunken revelers' attention because as long as the women have big boobs and a nice bum, that's all they care about in their drunken state. Everyone in this industry is under no illusion that the punters come to watch dancers like us for one reason alone. It's a grimy way to make money, but the women I dance with are some of the nicest, most down-to-earth and intelligent women I've ever met in my life. Our motto is, "If the booty can pay, then shake it away."

This reality I find myself in is a far cry from my younger childhood days where it had always been a dream of mine to dance professionally for big stage productions and in ballet shows such as *Swan Lake*. When I was growing up, I actually got to experience a taste of what real professional dance coaching was like. My grandparents had managed to scrape enough pennies together to be able to enrol me to take classes at Busy Bee's, a very sought-after dance academy which is still run today by the infamous owner, Marie Adams, aka *'The Dragon Lady'*. The students were mainly private school students, which made making friends… *difficult*, especially as I was in no uncertain way seen as *'Lower Class'*. After all, I went to a public school with a bad rep and lived in a rundown apartment block. None of the mums wanted their 'little darlings' associating with me outside of class. Perhaps they thought I'd be a bad influence and they'd have been right; I was always in and out of detention and lacking concentration in class. Dance was all I cared about; nothing else mattered.

Marie allowed me to keep my position within her dance school, but only because I was very skilled and each term could be paid for. Alas, when my grandfather passed away, Mum had to organise putting my gran into a home, as she'd developed dementia and needed round the clock care. I received a small inheritance fund which I'd planned to use for continuing my dance studies at Busy Bee's, but unfortunately, the old block of apartments my mum and I had been living in had a bad fire which resulted in a few deaths. And, as we had nowhere to go, I had to use all the money from the inheritance fund to get us to where we are now. If we had waited on the council to re-house us, we could have ended up living in a hostel for up to three years! At least this way we were in our own space (however small) and at least it was clean.

While in the shower, I ponder on my 'same shit-different day' living situation before stepping out, rapidly towelling myself dry, as the air around me is very cold and the heated towel rail gives little to no comfort from it. My waitressing garb, hanging on the towel rail to warm up, consists of a plain white shirt, black trousers and flat black shoes. Given how bad the weather is today, I put my work shoes in a plastic carrier bag and don my floral Wellington boots for the walk to work. I apply some very simple daily make-up in record time before leaving the bathroom and see Mum has already gone to work.

I quickly peek in the fridge and freezer to check on our food situation. You would have thought with my mother working in a supermarket it may prompt her to remember to keep food in the fridge and freezer, but *oh no*—not my scatty-brained mother. Depression has clung to her like an invisible unwelcome visitor for as long as I can remember. It became much worse after my grandfather's passing and then diagnosis of my grandmother's dementia, which followed into a rapid deterioration. Doctors considered it was probably brought on much faster from the shock of my grandfather's death.

Every day, I worry about Mum when I'm at work, as there was one day (referring now back to my earlier comment about being thankful that anywhere decided to take my mum on for full-time employment) as she had tried to end it all by taking pills she bought off some weirdo on a street corner. Fortunately for both of us, though, having never done recreational drugs up until that point, she had unknowingly bought and taken a non-lethal dose of a hallucinogen. She was found by police in a very high-end restaurant, dancing semi-naked on top of a bride and groom's top table, singing her heart out and murdering the lyrics to "Highway to Hell." This was after having wrestled the microphone midway through the wedding party's best man's speech. Guests took many, many photographs and videos of the incident, and it spread through the internet like wildfire. I have still never been able to bring myself to re-open my social media accounts to this day as, unfortunately, one of the guests had been a top editor for a big newspaper firm. So, my mum ended up splashed all over the front of said newspaper as *The Crazy Wedding Crasher*. Not our finest hour. I think (and secretly hope) it has permanently scared her straight. Doctors and therapists have helped, but I still don't feel I can ever completely trust her not to do something so stupid again. It feels most days as if roles are reversed and I'm the parent.

Seeing we have enough food for the next few days, I breathe a sigh of relief, but I make a mental note on the meals I can make up before needing to do another food shop. Reaching into the freezer, I pull out the frozen leftover lasagne I made last week and leave it on the side with microwave instructions written down onto a post-it note so Mum can cook it after it's defrosted. I also add to the note that I will be out dancing before she gets in from work so not to wait up for me.

Leaving cat biscuits and fresh water out for Binks—who has still yet to make an appearance from his cat cave—I say a cheerful goodbye to him before stepping outside into the cold, shutting the door, which automatically locks behind me.

The walk to work is usually a short one, but due to an ever-increasing headwind and now torrential downpour, it takes me some time to reach Chef No. 9. The passing cars and buses splash me with wave after wave of freezing cold, filthy roadside water as they drive by.

When I finally make it through the front door of the restaurant, I reckon I must resemble something more akin to that of a drowned rat! My rain mac had done its best to shield me from the onslaught of pelting rain and waves of water, but it just couldn't compete, as it was shower-proof only, not monsoon-proof. I am now a quivering, soaking wet mess.

"Jesus! Look at what the cat dragged in!" Sarah, one of my colleagues and also closest friends, exclaims while hurrying over to me. She hands me the tea towel that is draped over her arm to help take some of the water out of my hair and dabs at my clothes with it.

"It's like a cyclone out there!" I cry.

"No shit! Did you feel like you were on *I'm a celebrity?*"

"Ha-ha! Very funny. I'd better go and freshen up before I catch hypothermia!" Sarah laughs at my expense. *Rude!* I think, playfully.

"There are some clean, dry shirts in the back. You'd better hurry; the customers will be here predictably on time," Sarah remarks, flicking me hard on my bum with the tea towel. I yelp in surprise and then we both burst out laughing.

"Ow! *Ooh,* I owe you for that one."

"I might enjoy it," Sarah pouts her lips before waving me off in the direction of the staff room.

Entering the room, I bask in the warmth from the heater and send a quick text to my mum to let her know I arrived at work safely, whereby she responds to also let me know she was safe at work. *Relief!*

I soak up a moment of stillness and warmth before grabbing a clean dry shirt from one of the spares we have in the back office. I proceed to whip off my soaking wet shirt and replace it with a nice clean, freshly pressed one. It's so warm inside the office so I steal as much time as possible to fully defrost.

My trousers are still damp from the rain. Attempting to dry them the best I can with the cold hand dryer in the toilets awakens my skin in fresh goosebumps. My long apron will cover most of the damp stain until it dries on its own, so I'm not too bothered about it, knowing it will dry quite quickly. I hang my wet shirt above the small staff room radiator, along with my rain mac, hoping they will dry out before the end of my shift.

After taking a breath to prepare myself for the day ahead, I step out of the comforting warmth of the staff office. As cool air now clings to me, I proceed to tie my apron on and fix my hair. I wince as I slip my feet out of my Wellington boots and into my flat, plain black work shoes before entering the main hub of the restaurant. My feet silently protest with each step from the pain of the blisters on my toes, along with the bruised ligaments and joints. This is caused by the extra dancing hours I've been putting in to ensure I get the maximum chance for tips. The undesired effect from over-dancing is beginning to really show itself, which I felt the moment my shoes were on my feet.

Being used to having pained feet and remembering Busy Bee's mantra of "Pride feels no pain," I internally say this to myself before going to join Sarah, who is now already serving a long line of regular coffee and bacon roll customers coming to collect their sustenance before heading out to work for the day. The restaurant offers different menu items, but the bacon rolls and coffee are, by far, our most popular items.

By the time lunch hour comes around, we have the second wave of energetic, hungry customers coming in for their well-earned lunch breaks. A lot of them are fancy business types who come dressed in stereotypical smart corporate business attire.

There are more staff appearing now—which is odd—but then I clock that we also have a celebrity gracing us with their presence. I recognise him immediately from dance magazines: Joshua Glass, owner of one of the most elite nightclubs shrouded in mystery in Central London called Pink Club. Mysterious because no one actually knows what goes on within its walls. One thing everyone *does* know, however, is that celebrities are constantly seen there, and pics are snapped of them arriving and leaving the club. However, no one, as of yet in its five years of existence, has leaked any photos or videos of what goes on inside. Occasionally, there have been rare TV or magazine interviews with Joshua Glass or other people linked to the club off location.

One of the only known dancers for Pink Club is a woman known in dance circles as 'Sapphire Blitz' but whose real name is Bella Fitzroy. Not much is known about her either, only that she was a disgraced former dancer for a famous singing girl group. She became infamous for puking all over the lead singer after what was suspected to have been a drink and/or drug fuelled night before the big gig at a festival. Pink Club picked her up after her stint in rehab, and she must be doing well for herself because, as far as anyone knows, she has remained employed there since they opened five years ago.

Having done much homework on Pink Club, I can also tell you that four years ago, Joshua's twin sister, Mimi Glass, disappeared. It was said that she was murdered by her ex-boyfriend. As the story goes, Mimi was kidnapped and held captive in a small cabin in the middle of the woods in a remote area. She heard some kids walking through the woods and caught their attention, calling through a small window and telling them to get help. When the police showed up, the cabin was empty, yet there appeared to have been a struggle…even drops of blood were found. After days of searching, a body was found half-buried in the woods, so badly maimed that no one could identify her. Something about the torn clothing told Mimi's family that it was, in fact, her. Police then declared her dead.

The case exploded all over the media until the trial was concluded.

Joshua seemed to disappear off everyone's radar, and yet, here he is now—sitting a few mere feet away from me, not realising that I must be one of his biggest fans.

I find myself completely star struck. Joshua is even better looking in the flesh than in magazines or on TV. My cheeks turn bright red and my pulse rate quickens. In the world of dance, Pink Club is a constant hot topic, and dancers are always keeping their ears to the ground for any up-and-coming dance auditions or opportunities. But, as of yet, no such opportunities have appeared. I would never flatter myself to ever imagine I'd even be good enough to dance there.

My heart now strains as daydreamed thoughts of what could have been float around inside my mind as I watch Joshua Glass schmooze with his friends and colleagues, one of which is a sharply dressed woman with bright pink hair. Thoughts of dancing for a club like Pink Club evaporate as quickly as they crop up as more tables start filling up. Back down to earth again, the grief of my crushed dreams weighing heavily on me, I change tack and busy myself by focusing on customer orders.

Extra staff members arrive on shift. My boss, Sam, has had to break out the big guns as a long line of fans and paparazzi repeatedly try to gain entry. Specialist security teams and police are now guarding the doors and setting up barriers between our establishment and the general public. This allows for just a trickle of people in at a time as opposed to the torrent that has been beginning to build up.

Speaking of torrent: the weather has also improved, which doesn't help to stem the build-up of more and more dance fans outside, salivating to get a rare glimpse, snap or autograph of Joshua Glass.

The extra pairs of hands are very much appreciated since I'm beginning to struggle with the pain in my feet. I feel as if nails are being driven into the joints of my toes. I wonder if I shouldn't call my boss at Lucifer's Haven to cancel my shift, but I know if I do, Mum and I will fall short with our rent this month, which we can ill afford to do as we are on our last warning as it is. No—I'll just have to dose myself up on painkillers and hope for the best.

"Watch it!" someone yells close to where I've just served a table their food. Inadvertently, this makes me jump, reflexively spinning around to see where the voice came from. The jumpy move brings pain shooting through my foot, causing me to stumble momentarily and wobble off balance, but I bump into something that helps me to steady myself. I realise too late it was another member of staff directly behind me, holding a tray of scalding hot drinks, which they then proceed to lose control of. Unbeknown to me, the drinks have been made specially to be 'extra hot' and I can only watch in slow motion horror as the contents are sent hurtling away from the intended table and sent instead on a completely different trajectory, going towards one Joshua Glass and company, whereby the 'extra hot' drinks spill all over Joshua Glass and the woman with the vibrant pink hair. She immediately proceeds to jump up, screaming in pain as she rips off her expensive looking pin-stripe suit jacket. One of the buttons pings off and hits another customer directly opposite who begins to scream, "OW, MY EYE! I CAN'T SEE—MY EYE!"

The pink-haired woman, now showing a revealing plain, silk blouse splashed with hot coffee, stands up and stares daggers at me. My colleague, I notice—the one who actually threw hot drinks over the pair—is nowhere to be found.

Joshua Glass seems to wince only slightly and raises his hand to indicate everything is ok. He then begins to reach for napkins and dabs at his now coffee-stained leg. This all seems to happen in mere seconds. On instinct, I grab a jug of iced water from the nearest table and throw it over both Mr. Glass and the pink-haired woman. She instantly stops freaking out and just stands there, mouth agape, as she is now gasping from the shock of the cold water (ice bucket challenge comes to mind). She looks similar, I now imagine, to how I looked on arriving at work this morning, except she has wet tendrils of pink hair as opposed to my blonde hair.

Mr. Glass's bodyguard rushes up from behind, shoving me forward, and I'm too late to hear Sarah's warning shouts before I'm rugby tackled and sent sprawling straight towards Mr. Glass. My head crashes into his firm—and now iced-coffee-soaked torso—leaving me on my knees in a most un-lady-like position. Customers begin applauding, laughing, and wolf-whistling while taking photographs.

Joshua Glass sits as still as a statue, but the pink-haired woman—having now caught her breath—straightens up, giving me another *drop dead* look before proceeding to storm out of Chef No. 9. She is swiftly followed by other members of their party.

Mr. Glass says nothing, and I'm too afraid to look up at him. I am paralysed by embarrassment as the big burly security man helps me to my feet, apologising and asking if I'm ok. I'm shaking like a leaf from the shock and embarrassment.

Without speaking, I nod and run off to the safety of the staff room. I can hear the distant laughs, whoops and camera clicks of customers still going on as I flee, wishing the ground could swallow me up.

~ *Chapter 2* ~

"Oh, hi, darling. I thought you would be out already," my mum greets cheerily as she enters our apartment and hangs up her coat. "Ooh, lasagne, how lovely. Are we going to share this?" she continues, having seen my post-it note on the fridge.

"Hmm...oh, yeah. I had a migraine so came home early. Guess I'd better get my butt into gear for my night shift." I realise time is marching on and I had better start moving.

"I'm sorry to hear that, darling. Are you sure you're up for dancing tonight?" Mum asks, her brow furrowing in the middle.

Clearly, she hasn't seen the news!

"Well, the rent is due, and we can ill afford for me to lose a night of wages and tips. I've taken some pain relief, so I will be fine." I wasn't even believing the lie myself, as my feet hurt worse than they have felt in ages.

A pained expression crosses my mother's face, and it makes me feel awful for having been so blunt with her. But after such a crap day, I give myself a bit of a break. "Tell you what. I am free tomorrow evening. How about once I finish my shift at Chef No. 9, we go out for the evening? Maybe catch a movie and have some comfort food?" I offer, trying to lighten the mood and unburden myself in the process. The pangs of guilt I feel are now pressing upon me for being so catty towards my mum.

"Yes, alright then. That's a lovely idea. Hang on, let me grab my purse," Mum says, going to get a coin from her purse in the kitchen.

It is a time-honoured tradition that we both pick a movie when there are two big features that we both really want to see, but we have opposite film interests. This time, I want to watch the new comedy cartoon film, "Flozzy & Bonce" which is about a young girl, Flozzy, who—after experiencing bullying in school for being short—is comforted by a dog named Bonce that her parents bought her. My mum, however, is a real heartthrob romantic and wants to see the new Joan Wilderness movie, "Hearts and Flowers." It's a film about a war hero coming home to find his wife has had an affair and a baby while he's been at war, yet her new lover died, so he must now decide whether or not he will go back to her and help raise this child she had out of wedlock.

Mum and I flip the coin and call out "heads or tails." Once the coin is in the air, we run a circuit around our small lounge area, high fiving each other as we spin around the sofa before coming back to where the coin has landed. Loser pays for the movie and the winner pays for the food, so in a way it is really win-win.

"Ready...set...go!" Mum shouts as we both set off on our little run about the lounge. The pain in my feet is all but making me pass out, but I just manage to hide the crushing level of pain I'm in. We high-five each other and discover tails has won. Looks like we're in for a fun night of "Flozzy & Bonce."

I head for the bathroom once my mum has booked our tickets online and we agree on where we are going to eat for the night. I run a nice hot bath with Epsom salts and take my first dose of strong pain killers. I don't rely on them too heavily, as I've always been worried of addiction, so I only take them when absolutely necessary.

I then get to work treating and wrapping my feet. Normally, I'd be wearing high pole-dancing heels, but tonight I'm opting for my flat black ballet pumps. It may mean less tips as a result of losing my sexy edge with my pole-dancing shoes, but it's a necessary sacrifice if I am ever going to make it through tonight's show.

Binks is purring away happily on my bed. I sit down while I wait for the bath to fill, which doesn't take long. With the drama of the day still very fresh in my mind, I lie back and stroke Binks for a short while which helps to calm my nerves down. Eventually the bath is full, so I make my way into the bathroom. The hot water briefly stings my feet as I get in, but the salts and pain killers are soon working their magic and it enables me to fully relax. My mobile rings and I ignore it, knowing my voicemail will pick up anything urgent.

After thirty minutes of relaxation, I begrudgingly drag myself out of the bath and begin getting my things together for the night ahead. I'm opting to wear my silver hot pants, fluorescent pink leg warmers and pink body suit with black zebra stripes. I'm also opting for my black cowgirl hat that has diamantes on it which I sewed on. My black ballet pumps also have diamantes on and will be a darn sight more comfortable tonight than my torturous pole dancing heels. I throw my comfy strawberry tracksuit bottoms on and matching hoodie, packing

16

my hat and pumps into my bag. It's still pissing down with rain, so I've got my Wellies back on. I've been able to bandage my feet and put thick socks on and they don't hurt so much now.

I remember to check my phone and find there is indeed a voicemail on there, but just as I'm about to listen to it my ride arrives. Dante, my street dance teacher and friend, has come to pick me up. He is also a doorman at Lucifer's Haven and helped to get me the gig there. He knocks on the door, and I let him in briefly as I say goodbye to my mum before heading out. Binks has appeared and saunters over to sit with Mum on the sofa. I leave them both watching TV, the image I find to be endearing, as I head on back out into the cold with Dante.

~ *Chapter 3* ~

"How has your day been?" I ask Dante as we descend the stairs.

"Not bad. Yourself?" he replies while still walking ahead.

"Err…yeah, well, it was certainly different to most other days," I respond, knowing how cryptic I'm sounding.

"Why's that?"

We reach the bottom of the stairwell and aim for the door. Dante is tall and muscular. He has a mop of dirty blonde hair and has the most piercing blue eyes I've ever seen. Our friendship is more on a professional footing, as he is my dance teacher and we work together at Lucifer's Haven, but it doesn't hurt to recognise he is one stunning specimen of the masculine kind. I'm also not very trusting of men since a bad breakup two years ago when my ex-boyfriend put me in the hospital. I haven't dated anyone since and, for now, I'm happy on my own.

"Oh, nothing. Just that Joshua Glass graced us with his presence."

Dante stops fast, causing me to bump into him when I mention Joshua's name. "Sorry. Come on, let's go. Traffic is going to be bad, and I want to get there in plenty of time," Dante says, a bit more moodily than usual. He seems distracted, and I take heed to perhaps keep small talk to a minimum.

We sit mostly in silence in Dante's black Belair Chevrolet that he had brought over from the states. I wonder if it's challenging to drive a left-handed vehicle in the U.K., but the question dies on my lips as Dante seems to become increasingly tense while we now sit in mainstream traffic.

Cher's "Do You Believe in Love After Love" is quietly playing through the radio. A gentle rain begins to tickle the windows with a light tapping sound, and I find it only remotely soothing against the mounting pain in my head from a migraine.

"Hey, you ok?" I gingerly press as the swearing from Dante to other drivers reaches a whole new level on the road rage scale.

"I've got some personal shit going on at the moment. Sorry if I'm cranky. It's just…well…the truth is, my dance classes may get shut down. A big company wants to come in and buy the community centre where I currently teach. I can barely afford the rent for the space as it is, and…well, it may be the case that yet another much loved community space gets ripped down to create another sodding block of flashy apartments." Dante sighs heavily as if this admission has taken all the heat out of him.

"Then we will wage a protest to keep it open –"

"It will do no good, I'm afraid. It's council-owned. I've seen this happen too many times. If I can't teach, I am going to lose the only other source of income I have. It's a fuck pig, that's for sure."

"It would be a tragedy to lose your classes. Well, I hope you can come up with an alternative," I say somberly, knowing that there really is nothing to say. He is right: the council and big corporate companies do tend to win these things.

We arrive at Lucifer's Haven ahead of tonight's night shift. Dante parks the car in an underground carpark adjacent to the nightclub. I remember again to check my voicemails as Dante turns off the ignition and hands me the keys, reminding me to lock the car once I'm done and to give him back his keys. I nod to let him know that's affirmative.

"Darla! Darla…man, I hope you get this before you come for your shift tonight. It seems you have become a bit of a celebrity after an incident at your day job. Anyway, the place is teeming with tabloid press and the media so don't come here," my boss Chris says in a rushed message.

I all but drop my phone before I see Dante running—no…wait, correction, *sprinting*—back towards the car.

"What the –"

"We're leaving *right now*," Dante snaps. He switches on his ignition and speeds out of the carpark. Before I can say boo to a goose, we are heading back the way we came.

"Goddamn it, Darla, your face is apparently plastered all over news channels and the internet. Now I'm going to miss my shift –"

"As am I!" I interrupt in my defence.

"What the hell happened?"

"Let me explain over coffee…Angel Cake?" I suggest, hinting that we should go to our favourite café.

Dante agrees, and as he drives, I check online chatter. "Holy shit balls! You were not kidding! Those bastards! They are calling me 'blow job girl!' And some fuckers have even given my name to the press and where I LIVE! You don't think they'll –"

"Be at your apartment block? Yep, that's exactly where they will be. I suggest you stay at mine tonight," Dante snaps. I sense it's not up for discussion.

I quickly dial in my mum's number but there is no answer. "My mum…she isn't answering." I worry my bottom lip and hope to God she hasn't tried to kill herself out of sheer embarrassment this time.

"Ok…keep trying to get hold of her. What do you want to do?" Dante sighs and sounds increasingly fed up.

"Can we go back to mine? I know a back way into the building…oh, hi, Mum, it's Darla," I say, wondering why she has answered the phone giggling uncontrollably.

"Wait—Mum…do you have a *man* over?"

"Hello…Darla…hello…?" My mum fake a hangs-up, pretending like she didn't hear me when I know full well what's she's up to. I try to call her back, but I only get the sodding machine.

"Son of a –"

"Family issues? Come on. Angel Cake first then back to my place," Dante says, getting no argument from me. I just pray that whoever my mother's guest is won't accidentally let Binks escape.

~ *Chapter 4* ~

Angel Cake, a bookstore come café, is nice and quiet. I much prefer to buy and read my books here when I'm on my own. The owners of the café are Frank and Vera, a married couple who have been running the business for around ten years. I only know this because I worked a summer job here for them when Mum and I first moved to the area. They helped me with my job application for Chef No. 9 and have always been kind towards me.

"Hi, Darla. How are you, sweetheart?" Vera greets while giving me a welcoming hug.

"I've had better days, but nothing I'm sure a slice of your famous cherry pie and strong coffee can't sort out," I admit, almost salivating at the mere thought of Vera's homemade cherry pie.

"I'll get that right away for you. And what can I get for you, Dante?" Vera asks, looking at the pair of us conspicuously. I imagine she is wondering why we are not an item yet.

"Just a coffee for me, please. How's Frank?" Dante asks her.

I take my chance at the distraction to go and sit down in a hidden nook at the back of the café where there is warm, dim lighting surrounded by a few of the bookshelves. I melt into one of the soft, brown leather chairs and take a moment to ponder on my predicament. My feet feel as if they appreciate being able to take a load off. My migraine has also helped to take the pain away from my feet, since all I can now feel and concentrate on is the dull and constant 'thud-thud-thud' of my pulse as it pounds away painfully on the right side of my brain. I really am in no fit state to be doing any kind of dancing, so I am thankful that I have been given the night off. Chris assures me that I will still be paid, which is a relief.

Dante eventually approaches with our tray of goodies. Vera has treated us both to complimentary finger sandwiches as well as some slices of her famous cherry pie.

"Thank you, Vera. That is very kind of you," I call out. She nods in response before going about clearing and cleaning the other tables.

"It looks like the press have left your apartment building. Everyone now seems to be discussing the other breaking news story to do with Pink Club," Dante tells me. I can tell he's trying to pique my interest, but my headache is in full swing now.

There is a small TV near the serving counter, and I all but nearly choke on the bite of cucumber sandwich in my mouth as I see the news headline: *Bella Fitzroy has been found dead in her apartment after a cocaine drug overdose.*

"I now see your point about the press moving on to bigger news," I tell Dante, pointing ahead to the TV screen.

"Yes, it seems she had been hiding this drug habit, and after one wild night in her apartment she took one sniff too many and snuffed it—pun intended," Dante says, jokingly.

"How can you joke about this?" I accuse, horrified to see this side to Dante I wasn't accustomed to.

"There is something not many people know about me, Darla, and that is…I know Joshua Glass…personally."

"You're…he's…you're…GAY?" I sputter. My head now literally feels like it might explode.

"Don't be daft. I'm not gay and neither is he. We went to the same performing arts school. Joshua and Mimi were the top dancers of our year. We used to dance and hang out. I knew their leading choreographer, Octavia Perez, well. But…when we left college and moved on, a small troupe of us decided to stay together. We had an idea to set up our own dancing venture and then Mimi came up with the idea for Pink Club. We didn't have anywhere near the amount of money required to start a project like that, so we looked into loans and alternative options. We thought we were making headway, then everything went quiet. Joshua and Mimi dropped off radar for a while and then out of nowhere, Pink Club appeared.

"Me and some of the other dancers had been completely ghosted—dropped like a sack of potatoes when clearly something bigger and better came along. There is no love lost there between us, which is why I will not feel bad about their present bad luck situation." Dante explained it all quite coolly and I'm all but melting on the floor with the overload of information I've just been fed.

We sit in silence for a while as I digest everything. Suddenly, I feel an overwhelming sense of nausea from my worsening migraine. "I'm just going to pop to the loo before we have to go," I mumble, making a hasty exit. I walk quickly to the ladies' room but not so fast as to make people think I'm about to poo myself.

Once inside, I proceed to vomit up my cherry pie and other contents of my stomach. The pain in my head is excruciating and I am in desperate need for painkillers again. I clean myself up and then walk back into the main hub of Angel Cake.

"Are you alright, Darla? You look like you have seen a ghost," Vera observes, meeting me halfway. Her arms are loaded with trays of crockery ready for the dishwasher.

"Yes, I'm ok. You don't happen to have any paracetamol, do you? I've got one awful headache."

"I'll be right with you. Let me just take this to the kitchen –"

"Give me the trays," I demand kindly, finding it hard to watch the poor woman struggle.

"Thank you," Vera sighs with relief. "Since Frank injured his knee after a bad fall on a patch of ice, he's been a bit…well, you know…slow."

I relieve her of the heavy tray and walk swiftly into the kitchen. My heart swells with emotion at the couples' predicament. I wish I could come back to work for them, but the job just doesn't pay enough.

"Here you go, sweetheart." Vera hands me the painkillers and a glass of water which I thankfully swallow.

"Thank you ever so much. You're a life saver."

"It is no bother at all. Well, I had better get back to it. Hope to see you back here again soon," Vera says cheerfully. Then she walks back out to begin serving the last lot of customers before closing.

Dante and I leave Angel Cake, but thoughts of Vera and Frank weigh heavily on my mind.

~ *Chapter 5* ~

"Do you still want to crash at my place, or shall I take you home?"
Dante asks.

I am *so* tempted to take him up on his offer to go back to his place,
but I decline. "No, it's ok. I'll go home. Mum will just worry if I don't,"
I say, knowing full well my mother probably wouldn't even consider
until at least the following morning if I were still alive and well.

"Ok, your place it is then."

We arrive back at my apartment block and I'm thankful the
paracetamol Vera gave me is working its magic. I invite Dante up for
coffee and my heart does a little flip flop of happiness when he agrees.
*I really do fancy the pants off him, so any length of time in his company is always
time well spent,* I think.

"Hi, Mum. I'm back again. Are you alone?" I ask, peeping my head
around the door before deciding to enter fully. The last thing I want to
see is my mother and a strange man in their birthday suits doing a sexy
tango between the sheets. There is no answer, and all the lights are off.
My heart then does flip flops for a completely different reason.

"Something is wrong," I mumble to Dante, who seems to have

also picked up on the vibe that something is amiss.

"I'll go in first," Dante offers. I step aside to let him in.

"Yo! Darla's mum...you here?" Dante shouts. Again, no answer.

"Maybe she went out," I wonder as I enter the apartment, feeling cautious and spooked.

"It's ok. I found the answer as to where your mum is!" Dante shouts from the kitchen area.

"Pardon?"

"Says right here on this note: 'Hey D, gone to Paris for a mini break with John. Back soon. Thanks for the lasagne; it was very nice. Speak soon, love Mum.'"

I guess Flozzy & Bonce will have to wait! My blood is now beginning to simmer but I'm too exhausted to vent. I then remember our emergency money jar and, just as I expected, the money is all gone. Rolling my eyes, I decide enough is enough.

"That's it; I'm out. Do you mind if I stay with you until I can get another apartment—*for* myself and *by* myself?" I ask, stressing the last part of that sentence.

"You're really bailing on your mum this time?" Dante raises his eyebrows.

"I'm just tired, Dante. I need space and a place to call my own. I can't baby my mother anymore; I need to strike out by myself."

"Ok, but I'll have to ask you to pay towards food and board," Dante says.

My hero, I think as I agree on Dante's terms. I then begin to storm away from my old home as fast as my legs will carry me.

"What about your belongings?" Dante calls out. I suddenly

remember I haven't packed anything and I also—*to my horror*—realize that I was about to leave Binks behind. "Go and warm the car up. I'll be five minutes."

Dante does as instructed while I get to work, rapidly cramming clothes and essentials into a duffel bag. A little meow from the corner of my bedroom alerts me to where Binks is situated. Carefully placing him in his carry case, and checking I have everything I need, I walk out, shutting the door behind me. I post the keys through the letter box on my way out, not bothering with a note.

I had worked hard to save that emergency money, and off my mother goes, gallivanting willy nilly with the first waif and stray to offer her a *'good time'* with plenty of freebies such as a mini holiday. (Not into serious relationships, my mother only goes for men who come with perks before she bins them.) This really is the final straw and, in a way, I feel as if I want to shake Mr. Glass's hand for choosing today to wander into Chef No. 9, which inadvertently turned my day into the biggest shit storm to date. However, it also woke me up to the fact that I simply can't continue to live like this any longer. Something has got to give, and it appears it's me leaving my mother up to her own devices.

"You know, I really do feel I should charge you extra for bringing your small furry charge along as well," Dante says jokingly.

I almost miss the fact that it's meant to be a joke because of the anger now brewing inside my mind. "Oh…sorry…I forgot to ask if it would be ok –"

"Darla, will you *please* relax? While you were packing, I put out some feelers for anywhere that I can move my classes to, and it appears there is, in fact, a local leisure centre called Everest Fitness who can lease one of their dance studios to me by the hour. I have an appointment tomorrow with the agent and wondered if you'd like to come along as well."

"That was fast work, but at last some good news. Ok, I'll tag along. I'm on an early shift at Chef No. 9, so I will be finished by early afternoon. I'll help out but only if you give me a few free one on one lessons as a thank you."

"Sure, it would be my pleasure to give you some free dance tuition."

"Yay! Oh, hang on—Chris is calling." Our boss's number from Lucifer's Haven pops up on my mobile screen. "Hey Chris. Right...ah...tomorrow night...double pay? Are you sure? Erm," I look at Dante who is nodding furiously at me. "Ok, I'll come in. You're welcome, bye."

"Your luck seems to be changing. New place, double pay...*free* lessons from *Moi*. Yes, you can still have some freebies even though it now looks like I'm going alone tomorrow."

"Do you know something? I think you're right! My luck really *is* changing. And you want to know something else? It feels so *gooooood*," I laugh while celebrating in the passenger seat.

I check my phone again, but no message from my mum. Reality starts to sink in that she doesn't appear to really care much about me at all. As the thought crosses my mind, the short-lived burst of revitalised zest for life I'd just felt floats out as fast as it had floated in. I am, once again, left feeling deflated. Surely, there must be more to life than this.

29

~ *Chapter 6*~

Eva Godstone sits at her desk in her office, unsure how to navigate this latest predicament facing Pink Club. It was maxing out her PR skills, and her patience had long since run out.

Eva's office is decorated in a soothing palette of creams and mochas, which are carried through in the accessories and furniture. But no matter how relaxing her office is, or how comfortable her top-of-the-line orthopedic massaging desk chair feels, it won't help her deal with the tsunami of stress she's currently experiencing. Her voice mail box is full; the emails and voicemails continually pouring in. There are condolence messages from fans of Bella, then there is the hate mail from the not-so-big fans.

The celebrities booked in for the spring gala have had their PR teams hound Eva for all information regarding the gala and ensuring they can get refunds if required. Joshua assures her that the gala will still be going ahead and that he has faith in her to be able to find a new leading dance lady within the short space of time she now actually has to find said person.

The press stood outside as long as they dared until the weather made it unbearable even for them. Eva made a brief statement, telling everyone that Joshua was unavailable for any comment but that they would make an announcement on their own social media pages as soon as they had any more information to share.

Delivery personnel had been coming and going with flowers and gifts of condolences from celebrity guests that frequented Pink Club often and also by people in high society dance circles who had known Bella personally. Eva had needed to coordinate a dance studio to store everything that kept arriving. Some of the gifts included huge teddy bears that she already decided to donate to a local children's charity. Max Adams, their chief of security, had been busy making security checks on all delivery personnel and packages. It certainly hadn't been a slow day.

Octavia Perez takes a moment to breathe before knocking and entering Eva's office with fresh lattes, noticing Eva looks a sorry sight indeed. *Lack of sleep does not sit well on her face,* Octavia thinks, observing the very dishevelled woman sitting in front of her who is normally otherwise very sharply dressed and well-groomed.

"Woman, when are you going to get your butt back home?! You look like the walking dead!" Octavia exclaims. She places the cardboard holder with their coffees gingerly on Eva's desk which is littered with stacks of papers, contracts, and a plethora of junk food wrappers. Eva recoils momentarily as the memory of hot coffee spilling all over her wakes her up far quicker than the caffeine laden drink now on her desk ever could.

"In truth, you're right; I *am* exhausted. I've just had one of our highest esteemed clients on the phone asking for yet more assurance that the spring gala is *still* going ahead, and I've had to lie through my teeth to tell them it most certainly *is* and that we have a special act not to be missed! I'm not very good at lying at the best of times, but when it's to Arabian royalty it's a whole new level of insanity. I have zero contingency plans for us if we don't find someone new...and fast. The whole thing could fall apart, and I'll never get a job working PR again after this stunt. My career, your career—heck, *all* our careers—will be down the drain, and I can't afford to let that happen. Sometimes I feel like I can't breathe, and I –"

"Ok, ok. Look at me...good. Now I want you to breathe out. One...two...three...and in. One...two...three...hold, and out. Now, have a sip of your coffee," Octavia instructs, helping Eva return to a calmer state of mind.

"Thanks, V. You are always so good at bringing me back down to earth."

"Don't mention it. I'd better go and put the backup dancers through their paces. And Eva...don't sweat it. I've got my best people on the case, looking for new talent out there as we speak," Octavia reassures, gaining a wan smile from a shattered Eva. "Get some rest. I'll see you tomorrow."

It is the briefest of moments before someone else comes to interrupt Eva. "Knock, knock. Only me," Max says cheerfully.

"*Please* tell me it's not another flower or gift delivery, Max. We're fast running out of room! We could open our own flower shop at this rate!" Eva cries, rubbing her face.

"Man alive, Eva, you look like hell. When did you last sleep?" Max sounds both annoyed and concerned.

32

"Don't worry. I've told V that I am going to get some sleep. I'm dead on my feet anyway and am no good to anyone in this state."

"Just make sure you *do* rest up; I need everyone here in tip top shape to keep us all safe. If you're this exhausted, you could make a mistake and let *who knows* inside," Max tells her as a friendly warning and reminder.

"You're right," Eva agrees, having a big yawn. "Actually, I think I'll knock off now. The emails can wait a few hours longer for me to sort through them."

"That sounds like a wise decision. Can I drive you home?"

"What about *his majesty?*" Eva asks sarcastically, inquiring to the whereabouts of Joshua.

"Ah…yes. That is what else I've come to tell you. He's now flown to Tuscany to see his mum and dad. I sent a different team with him, as it was his request that I stay to help keep an eye on things here."

"Of course—Mimi's birthday…right. I should be off. A lift would be great, thanks." Eva grabs her coat and coffee before being escorted by Max to one of the company cars.

~ *Chapter 7* ~

It has been a few days since I left my old apartment that I shared with my mother. Eventually, I received a text and voicemail from her. She appeared to sound happy, at least. I couldn't bring myself to tell her I'd moved out. I'm sure this new man, John, could pick up any rent owing, as I sure couldn't afford to keep up with my mother's pace and habit of spending my hard-earned money this way. I was done being the adult. It was time to step out on my own and this was the only way to do it.

Dante's apartment was a lot more spacious than mine had been. The walls—a classic old brickwork design—are adorned with his dancing competition trophies, awards and other paraphernalia. His kitchen has oak wood surfaces, and the whole apartment oozes masculine charisma. I'd be lying if I said I wasn't just a bit jealous of the female companions he would undoubtedly bring back here from time to time, as he didn't appear to have a permanent female fixture to which he calls "girlfriend."

I have my own bedroom that is actually bigger than a broom closet, and I have a DOUBLE BED! I think the only time I have ever slept in a double bed was when my grandparents would take Mum and I away for long weekends or summer holidays abroad and we would stay in a nice villa or hotel.

My heart swells at the memory of my grandparents and how they were a constant in my life while I was growing up. My dancing classes were the best gift from them to me because—even though things haven't panned out how I'd hoped—I still got to experience what it was like to dance at one of the best dance schools in London and no one can take that away from me.

"Hey, are you ready to go? Our shift starts in two hours." Dante pokes his head around my bedroom door. Correction…'temporary' bedroom door—like almost everything in my life that's temporary these days.

"Yeah, I'm ready." Binks is asleep at the foot of my 'temporary' double bed. He looks so cute when he's sleeping.

"How are your feet feeling today?"

"Much better, thank you," I answer, doing a mini pirouette in Dante's kitchen space to make my point.

"Cool, cool. Right, come on, then. I want to beat rush hour traffic. It's pissing down out there so you may want to grab a coat."

I decide to don my only and ever-faithful rain mac with my flowery Wellington boots, putting my comfy trainers in my changing bag. My costume includes silver pole dancing shoes with clear, see-through heels now that my feet are feeling better.

Dante was not kidding when he said it was pissing down. Thankfully, he has parked in the basement area of his apartment block so we won't get rained on as we leave, but the car park nearest to the entrance of Lucifer's Haven is outside, which will expose us to the elements until we reach the doors at the back of the nightclub that is for staff only.

I always wear a mask when I dance at Lucifer's Haven so it keeps my identity a bit of a mystery. I have colleagues from Chef No. 9 who sometimes come to the club for a dance and to unwind who know it's me, but for anyone else I'm a mystery. We are all assigned a bouncer at our individual dancing stations and a makeshift barrier now sits between our individual stages. These extra measures were made after a man went for one of the girls with acid. It turned out the woman had declined this man's offer for going for a drink after one of her shifts here, and he sought revenge by coming back on another night with acid. But the acid ended up all over himself and the hand of one of the bouncers who wrestled him to the floor after recognising the guy was carrying a strange object just moments before the attack. The dancing girl left, and, like buses, another one was soon signing up to dance for money. We are very expendable here and no one's job is 100 percent secure, which is always in the back of my mind.

"Right. Now, before we head inside, I have a proposition for you," Dante speaks, looking at me squarely with a serious expression on his face.

My pulse quickens and I feel myself blushing. "Now, hang on a second here, Dante. I know I'm temporarily living with you, but –"

"Would you like to stay at mine more long term? The truth is, I could really use the help with the rent," he interrupts, thankfully saving me from well and truly putting my foot in my mouth.

"I'd love to. Wow, yes, of course. Thanks so much." I throw my arms around Dante's neck before I can stop myself.

When I sit back in the passenger seat, there is the briefest moment of awkwardness, and then Dante jumps out of the car. He jogs around to the passenger side, holding his umbrella, and helps me out. My heart sings on how chivalrous the man is. I then worry about the blurring of lines between professionalism and personal, seeing as we now live under the same roof.

~ Chapter 8~

The dressing room is alive with the familiar buzz of excitable energy as the other women doll themselves up to look as raunchy and tantalisingly sexual as possible. Sex sells, after all. A lot of the women here have afforded to have 'enhancements' done to certain parts of their anatomy, which certainly earns them bigger tips.

The overpowering smells of deodorants, hair and body sprays, and perfumes mix to make an extremely toxic—almost suffocating—aroma inside, so I am thankful my station is right next to the doorway. Of course, that means there is an occasional blasting of stale nightclub air every time someone enters or exits. It may not smell particularly pleasant, but it's easier to breathe through the body odour and orangey air freshener smell wafting in than this gas chamber of pure chemicals.

The music's already lively and the number of people is fast beginning to fill up the space inside Lucifer's Haven as we all prepare to dance the night away.

"Hey, Darla, how are you doing?" Bonnie, our eldest and most experienced pole dancing lady, greets, collaring me as I rapidly begin applying my makeup.

"I'm ok. Oh, shit! Is it a theme night tonight?!" I suddenly notice everyone else's costumes and I'm panicking that I have no costume ready.

"It's the 90's so don't sweat it." She turns to talk to the other girls. "Hmmm, Lucy...hand me your khaki shorts from safari week. Dee, I want your turquoise tank. Alexa, throw me your work boots." She collects what she asks for and turns to me. "There—now go get dressed into these. I'll fix your hair and makeup. Trust me, the guys are gonna love your look tonight."

I think she's completely lost her marbles, but I'm out of options, so I go and do as she instructs, thanking the other ladies for lending me their clothes. I don't know why on earth I've been asked to don Alexa's building work boots, but thankfully we share the same shoe size, so apart from the boots being just a tad too wide, they aren't uncomfortable.

"Bonnie, what about my pole dancing shoes? I'm not going to earn anything tonight dressed like this," I moan despairingly, as now I have no time to change.

The other women seem to have cottoned onto what Bonnie was up to and have been paying me compliments to my look, saying they wish they had thought of my theme, but I'm completely at a loss.

"I'm going to do your hair. Close your eyes. When I'm done and you open them, you'll hopefully get where I am going with this." Bonnie ushers another woman to the wig room.

"Oh, here, give her these as well," a voice that sounds like Alexa's says. I yelp in surprise as something cold and squishy gets pushed down the tank top.

"Boob enhancements. Good call, Alexa," Bonnie laughs as I become tempted to open my eyes.

After a bit more fussing, I can finally look in the mirror. My jaw almost hits the floor.

"See? Told you it would be fine. Now get your booty and boobies ready, Miss Croft," Bonnie demands, winking at me as she flattens down her Union Jack dress.

On my head is a real hair wig designed to look just like a British video game character. The look is finished with rose-tinted glasses and a belt of fake guns. I'm also wearing a pair of another dancing woman's fingerless biker gloves. Everyone's been so kind in coming to my rescue. They had all seen my ordeal at Chef No. 9 (for the briefest moment it existed in media and social media history, but none of them spoke of it), and I find the sentiment truly touching. Who would have thought that some of the most trustworthy people that I would meet— to date—would be a group of pole dancing ladies? It says it all when you can trust pole dancing friends more than you can trust your own mother.

"Ok, ladies, bring it in, bring it in," Bonnie commands like a pro, calling us all into a huddled circle. "Watch your backs, shake what your mother gave ya, and above all, have FUN and earn them big tips."

The room erupts into a short-lived burst of joviality before we all line up and are helped to our individual staging dance areas. The ladies wearing pole dancing shoes need extra help to get up onto the platforms by nightclub staff, and I'm thankful to have flat boots on for a change because at least it means I'll be dancing in relative comfort tonight.

Our DJ, Franz, clocks me and puts a special shout out to the nightclub's very own Cressida Croft, Crime Fighter. The club erupts in wolf whistles, cheers and feet stamping as the dance soundtrack to the video game plays loudly across the floor. Bonnie wasn't wrong; I certainly was drawing a lot of attention to myself.

As I start my dance routine, I'm grateful for being able to wear sunglasses on stage instead of a mask. They are more comfortable, and I can see more of the dance floor beneath and around me.

Dante is on door duty tonight, so I have other bouncers guarding my stage area. The crowd is a nice, lively bunch. Tips are put into containers tied to the mesh fencing, which keeps punters from getting too close after the attempted acid attack.

Bonnie catches my eye and blows me a kiss while winking at me. The tips are rolling in nicely, and requests have been put through to the bouncers for photo opportunities. It is a grace of the nightclub to reward our more well-behaved gentlemen the chance to have photos with their favourite ladies of any given evening. Some men come for stag do's and want mementos, and other times it's just single guys who just broke up with their girlfriends. Sometimes it's even ladies who fancy some of us! The club has made many friends of its regular customers over the years. Although sometimes fights break out and police have to be called, for a majority of the time people just come here to drink, dance, ogle the dancers and have a good time.

By the end of my first round of dancing, I decide to use my thirty-minute break to get a quick snack and a drink. Damion, one of the bouncers for my area this evening, lets me know at least ten guys have been granted a photo opportunity with me, which means a bit of extra cash—as well as tips (which are all split equally)—because when we get photos taken, we are given five pounds for each one taken. So, it looks like I have potentially an extra fifty pounds in my pocket from tonight's shift. I already decide that I will spend the money on a nice bouquet of flowers for my grandmother when I go to visit her this weekend in the home. She won't know who I am or what the flowers are for, but it's nice to be able to do something kind for her after her and my grandfather did so much for me growing up. I will undoubtedly cry after seeing her the way she is now, but visiting her regularly is the least I can do, especially with Mum being the way she is.

Thinking of my mother reminds me to check my phone to see if I have any messages or missed calls, but—surprise, surprise—I have nothing from her. Why, I ask myself, is it me worrying about her like a worried parent? Shouldn't this be the other way around? I think that as I re-enter the dressing room on my break where the toxic aroma is a bit less intense now that nothing has been sprayed in here for about two hours.

I enjoy the briefest moment of stillness before more ladies begin to come inside on their breaks. Bonnie sidles up to me giving me a knowing look. "See? I told you the guys would love your outfit," she says with her classic know-it-all smile and a glint in her eyes.

"Yeah, thanks. If only you could solve all my problems like a fairy godmother," I say exhaustedly.

"Oh, sweetie, things not so good? Come on; let's go to the upstairs office and you can tell me all about it." Bonnie gently pulls me out of my chair, and we make our way to the small office-come-staff room above.

"Thanks for the help tonight," I tell the other ladies just before we exit into the corridor to begin ascending the stairs.

~ *Chapter 9* ~

"Right, come along missy. What's eatin' ya?" Bonnie gets straight to the point

Seeing as we are alone upstairs, I relax enough to open up. "Where to start? Ok, so my mum ups and leaves for an impromptu holiday with her latest five-minute squeeze, without so much as a "bye," all the while having taken my hard-earned emergency cash, leaving me well and truly in the lurch. But then that was ok because I'm now actually bunking up with Da...a friend." I thankfully caught myself before revealing just who I was living with now. "But," I continue, "what I am most upset and angry at is the fact that I've had my face plastered all over social media with the seedy tabloids calling me 'blow job girl' after the hot drinks incident at my other job." I let out a big sigh of relief at getting it all off my chest.

"Baby girl, hear me and hear me good. We are all tired—*believe* me, we are—but don't let those things get you down. Family is...well *family* at times. But we are your family here, too. Hoes before Bro's, am I right?" Bonnie laughs at herself. "And don't forget, no publicity is bad publicity. It certainly got you out there with your name attached to only one of the most elite, most amazing up and coming nightclubs in London!" Bonnie says, grinning wildly at me.

I can sort of see her point, but the image forever burned of me on my knees with my face so close to Joshua Glass's crotch makes me feel embarrassed all over again.

"You always know just how to make me feel better," I say, genuinely feeling like a weight has lifted off my shoulders.

"Don't sweat the small stuff. I mean, look at me. I may be pushing forty, but I'm having the time of my life. I'm fit, I'm *damn* sexy, and I make my own money to support myself. If I can do that, you sure as hell can. You're twenty-four, baby—young, fit, and athletic. This job will NOT be your destiny forever.

"I know how badly you wanted to dance professionally; I've seen you sometimes in here rehearsing before work. You dance so beautifully, and nobody can take that away from you—not your mum, not work…heck, not even the *fabulous* Joshua Glass and Pink Club Posse. So, you just keep doing you and forget about everyone else. No one cares about the five-minute gossip section of tabloid mags and papers. People are now fixated on the death of that leading what's-her-face. There's always something better for the hounds and trolls to focus their attention on."

"Thanks so much for this, Bonnie. I really needed to talk, and I feel like I've taken a load off," I say, feeling some of the stress ebbing away.

We head to the staff kitchen area where I decide upon a slice of apple pie and cappuccino from one of the vending machines. Lucy and Alexa join us for our mini break before we have to get back out there

45

for the second half of our shift.

"So, tell me…did he smell good?" Bonnie asks, wickedly grinning at me, knowing just how *up-close* and *personal* I had gotten to Mr. Glass and his…nether regions!

"Mmm, he smelled really good like spice and all things nice," I reply, smiling back just as wickedly.

"Lucky cow," she says in jest.

We manage to eat our food and have our drinks in relative peace before the next half of our shift.

* * * * *

The Next Day

"Ok, time to get these audition applicants picked!" Eva says to herself, cracking her knuckles and loosening up her neck as she powers on her computer.

After about an hour, however, Eva is fast losing the will to live. All the applicants have barely any dance experience; they all seem to be fans who have poured in, applying to dance for Pink Club through the application form Eva put out on social media dancing platforms. It had stated in the advert that the application was for *professional dancers only,* but the tsunami of phonies now darkening her Inbox was too much for her to take.

The dance schools that Pink Club had connections with were all holding on tight to their own leading dancers, as they were the competition winners and made them the big bucks. Dancers who had moved on from their academics and schools were already enrolled in stage productions, cruise ships and other dancing projects.

"Shit! Shit! Shit! Damn you, Bella, and your cocaine habit. Eurgh! What am I going to do?" Eva shouts, while raking her perfectly polished pink nails through her just-as-pink and vibrant-coloured hair.

Deciding that waiting for a dancer to come to them was fruitless, and as the search had thrown up no one even remotely appropriate for the position, Eva decides to call Octavia to see if she has had any joy.

"Hey, V, it's me…listen, give me a call when you're free." Eva leaves a desperate sounding and hurried message on her friend and colleague's voicemail.

A small, plain black and white photograph of Mimi sits on Eva's desk. She is laughing and looks completely carefree and happy. Eva can't bear to look at her face, knowing the sorry state the club is in right now, so she places the photograph face down for the time being. There is nothing else for her to do today, so she decides to go for a run before getting a bite to eat.

Just as Eva begins her run, her phone rings to life, causing her to pause to answer it. "Hello, Miss Godstone speaking. Who is calling?"

"Eva it's me, V."

"Oh, sorry V, bit of a shit morning. I've made no headway with any potential dancers. How about you…any joy from the word on the streets?"

"Nothing as of yet, but…there may be someone I know that may be able to help us," Octavia says tentatively.

"Ok, spit it out. What's the 'but'?"

"He…was sort of ghosted by Joshua and Mimi and our dance troupe who set up Pink Club."

"No, forget it. No one with grief against us can be considered. It's too risky. We don't need any more bad press."

"Ok…I'll keep looking and keep my ears open. I will let you know as soon as I hear anything."

"Yes, please do. The moment you know something or of someone please tell me straight away."

"You got it. Ok, I'd better get back to it. See you later."

"Ciao, ciao," Eva says, hanging up the call, now feeling more increasing pressure at their predicament. Continuing her run, Eva thinks about alternative advertising routes.

~ *Chapter 10* ~

I awaken to the smell of bacon and smile, realising that Dante must be cooking us both breakfast. How lovely. Stretching and yawning, I say a sleepy good morning to my furry friend at the foot of my bed, who raises his head in recognition before going back for a snooze.

I tie my floral dressing gown together over my pale blue pyjamas and slip my feet into my oversized pink bunny slippers. I prepare to step out with my hair in typical bed hairstyle, but I don't care, as my tummy rumbles excitedly at the prospect of food. Probably more exciting is the fact I'll be dining with Dante—just the two of us.

Padding into the kitchen area, I find that Dante is nowhere to be seen. I do spot a few slices of fried bacon on the counter, and just off to the side of that on a bread board are two freshly buttered breakfast rolls. There's also a tray with fresh apple juice (my favourite; such a charmer.)

Deciding there is time, I make a mad dash back into my bedroom and head to the en-suite bathroom (yes, I also have an en-suite, don't you know) where I proceed to furiously brush my tangled mop of blonde hair before putting on the faintest amount of makeup while checking my morning breath. After giving myself a pep talk in the mirror, and bolstering my confidence, I head back out.

On re-entering the kitchen, I see that the tray has vanished. *Odd,* I think before hearing voices coming from Dante's bedroom. I creep down the corridor and notice his bedroom door is marginally ajar. I put my head close to the gap where the distinct sound of a woman's voice can be heard.

"I'll just go and get some fruit," this woman says.

Shit! I think, then speedily but quietly sprint back to the kitchen. I mess my hair up, wanting to make it look like I've just got up.

"Oh, hey, you must be Darla. My name is Felicity. I'm Dante's girlfriend." The bubbly and stunning species of female human reaches one of her perfectly manicured hands out to greet me. She is GORGEOUS! Legs for days, a mane of wavy brown hair, and a smile that has me instantly think of rainbows and sunbeams. If I wasn't straight, I'd *definitely* be a jealous lesbian.

Of course he'd have a woman like this, not a scrag end like me, I think as realisation punches me hard in the gut.

Suddenly, wanting to be anywhere but here in Dante's apartment, I look for any possible escape routes. My stomach growls loudly, betraying me and making an escape impossible now, as Felicity tells me to sit down while she makes me my very own bacon roll. The woman cooks—she must obviously be amazing in bed—and has everything going for her in the looks department.

"So…you and Dante are an item. He never mentioned having a girlfriend."

"The man loves being mysterious and is fiercely private. I've been

50

overseas doing relief aid work. It looks good on my resume and all the children at the camp in Nepal where we were helping to build a school are super cute and very welcoming. I'm thinking of going back again someday," Felicity says as she places fresh bacon rashers in the frying pan. I notice an accent to her voice and guess Italian. How can I be jealous of such a selfless angel that is this Felicity woman?

"It would appear he *is* very private. Well done on the relief aid work," I say with an overwhelming sense to get out of here as fast as possible. The last thing I want to be subjected to are all the 'sounds' that tend to happen when boyfriends and girlfriends get hot and heavy between the sheets.

Just like that, my crush bubble is well and truly burst. Maybe this is for the best. Now our relationship can remain purely professional. *Yes, it is really for the best…truly,* I think, trying my hardest to see the upside to this latest upset in my life.

"Thanks. Now, I don't want you to feel like you're intruding staying here, but…if *you* find it awkward, then maybe it would be better if you found somewhere to stay while I was visiting."

Great hospitality, Felicity. Bit rusty on the dismount, though. Aha! I found a flaw in her: her bedside manner could do with a bit of a polish. Not so perfect after all. The thoughts make my little green-eyed monster inside smile and twirl.

I hear her loud and clear, though, and can't blame her wanting me out of the way to have Dante all to herself. I'd probably be the same, to be fair.

"Yes, of course, no problem. You haven't seen each other and clearly need to catch up. Tell you what, I'll go and get my things

51

together and take that bacon roll to go if that's ok." I get up off the kitchen barstool and make a fast exit to the bedroom (no longer *my* bedroom—this has to be a record move for me.)

"Ok, I'll leave it on the side for you," Felicity calls out as I shut the door. I briefly put my hand back out to give her a thumbs up.

"Just as well I hadn't fully unpacked yet, aye, Binks?" I quickly change into a pair of jeans and t-shirt, throwing a hoodie over the top, and pull on a pair of thin thermal socks, adding my comfy walking boots. I've called a taxi and make sure I have enough cash to both pay for the fare and to leave something for Dante for allowing me to stay with him for a few days. My tips from the other night should cover the gesture. It is upon checking my financial situation that I also see on my phone that I have a missed call and message from my mum. Her message says: *Where are you? I've popped the kettle on.*

It is my day off from dancing, but I'm still to work the late shift at Chef No 9. I send a hurried response back to my mum, lying through my teeth, feeling both disappointed and despaired that I'm now going backwards and no longer forwards with my *new* life. The sense of feeling of failure makes me feel numb to my core.

Wild night at the club so spent the night with a friend, I reply so she doesn't worry—not that she *would,* knowing my mother.

Can you grab some milk on the way home? We're running low, is her response.

Sorry, Dante—looks like I'm going to have to owe you, I say to myself. I know I will now need to do an unexpected food shop, and after I pay the rent that I'd sworn I wasn't going to pay on that shitty apartment after my mother's latest antics, here I was breaking my own promise to myself, because—unlike her—I find it harder abandoning her the way she does me sometimes.

Binks is tucked away in his carry case, and my duffel bag is slung over my shoulder ready to go. Someone leaves Dante's bedroom, so I hot foot it out of there.

~ *Chapter 11* ~

It is not until I am downstairs that I realise I have left my purse on the kitchen countertop. I must have put it down when I grabbed the bacon roll off the side.

Fuck! is all I can think. There's no way I'm going back to collect it, but this means I can't pay for my taxi which is now sitting outside.

"Did you order taxi?" the Indian speaking driver says to me.

Shaking my head and pulling my hood up, I walk on by, feeling bad about wasting the man's time, but my pride now sees me with the prospect of having to walk a chunk of my journey home.

The weather has brightened up and the sun begins to break through white fluffy scattered clouds. My journey has taken me to Hyde Park, so deciding to take a load off, I wander inside its grounds and go towards the boating lake area. The ground is well kept and dry, and sitting on the earth feels good after being surrounded by concrete for most of my days.

There are families and tourists scattered about, and a pang of jealousy pain rips through me as I see a mother and father having fun with what I'm presuming is their child, taking a nice family stroll. The man is holding onto the little girl who has a pink bow in her hair. The woman is talking lovingly to the girl while they both smile and laugh before continuing their walk. It is then, when they move off, that I can see they have another daughter, probably about eight to nine years old, dressed in a pink ballet outfit, happily skipping along beside them.

I will, of course, never have that experience in my life, but I swear if I ever do meet my Prince Charming and am lucky enough to have children, they will be loved so much and be very much planned…not conceived on a one-night lustful evening, potentially in some shabby photo booth situated on the London Underground!

My phone breaks my reverie, as does Binks, who is now noisily meowing for his cat biscuits. Sighing, I go to answer my mobile and fancy that it's my adoring mother. Feeling nothing short of wanting to lob my phone into the boating lake, I swiftly answer.

"Darla? Where are you? Is everything alright?" my mum asks, actually managing to sound marginally worried on the end of the phone.

"Yes, Mum…I'm fine. Sorry, I decided to go for a walk."

"Darling, I have some dreadful news. Binks…well, he seems to have gone missing. I've been busy all morning getting missing cat posters together for you, and –"

"Its fine; he's here with me."

"Oh…well, that's a relief at least. Hang on a moment—do you mean to tell me that all this time I've been worried about Binks, and he's been with you?"

"Yes, Mum," I say, sighing.

"Why is Binks with you? I'm presuming he didn't go clubbing as well."

It is at this very moment that I see Dante. He looks stressed, like he has lost something, and I can see him placing his hands to his mouth, calling out. With my interest now piqued, and concerned as to why he looks so alarmed, I tell my mum I'll call her back and hang up. Using my fingers to whistle, I manage to grab Dante's attention. He looks flustered, and by the time he notices me and has jogged over to where I am, it takes a moment for him to catch his breath.

"I'm…glad…I…found…you," he says, panting.

"Oh—really?" I feel a tad confused.

"Phew! Ok, caught my breath back," he says, doubling over and taking a big breath in and out before continuing. "Felicity said you left. Knowing her, I knew you wouldn't have just got up and gone for no reason –"

"You mean your *girlfriend,* Felicity."

"GIRLFRIEND?! Felicity is NOT my girlfriend," Dante cries out, seemingly aghast at the notion.

"So, if she's not your girlfriend, then what exactly was she doing in your bedroom, *hmmm?*" I ask, feeling more confused than ever now.

"She is my ex-girlfriend. We bumped into each other at Lucifer's Haven, one thing led to another, and we just sort of ending up reminiscing about the 'good old-days,'" Dante says, now looking sheepishly at me.

"So, she doesn't work on projects helping to build a school in Nepal? And how did you find me anyway?" I asked, now more bemused than ever as to just how my friend-come-temporary-stalker had materialised.

"The Nepal thing is true, just not the girlfriend part. I used the find your phone thingy to find you. Remember you lost your mobile at the club a few weeks back? I found it using mine. I remembered your login password and just followed the little dot all the way here."

"Where is Felicity now, then?"

"She left, but not before I told her off for scaring you away. What a piece of work. I now see why we definitely wouldn't have worked out."

"Don't be too hard on her. She *is* helping people in devastated countries to build a school –"

"Yeah, only to boost her modeling profile where she can add "charity aid worker" to the list to help get her foot in the door for *'Hollywood'*—or so she thinks."

"Interesting to see your take on her now after what must have been a wild night between the sheets," I say, inwardly dying inside as the words leave before I can engage brain.

"Ha, ha! Oh, Darla, that imagination of yours is priceless. Felicity slept on the sofa. She tried to butter me up this morning with breakfast, but I wasn't having any of it. We're over, and she finally, I think now, understands that. I only let her crash here because she was sozzled, and her so-called-friends all left in cabs without her. I'm amazed you didn't hear us come in."

Yes! The man is still single, sexy and unattached. My inner sex goddess does a little boogie in my mind.

"I was really tired after last night's performance and sometimes I guess I sleep like the dead—or so my mother would say. Oh, *shit!*"

"What? What's the matter?" Dante asks, looking concerned.

57

"My mum—she's back and she's waiting for me at home."

"You haven't told her you moved out yet?"

"Well, that's just my point. I *thought* I had moved out, but then Felicity arrived and made me feel bad hanging around when she said she was your girlfriend. Then Mum texts me and says she's back, asks where I am and says she's putting the kettle on. I tell her I'm on my way back, and now…well, now what?" I prattle on, throwing my arms up despairingly.

"Ok, take a breath. Here is what we will do: you go and see your mum, and I will take Binks and your bag back to mine—don't look at me like that. You can't go back to living with your mum the way she is, Darla. She has to learn to stand on her own two feet."

"What about her suicide attempt? I mean, I know she said it *wasn't* a suicide attempt and that she just wanted to get high, but she can't look after herself."

"Trust me, your mum *will* be ok. Now go and break the news gently to her and I'll see you back at mine." Dante's tone suggests this is not an option. I know he is right; I am never going to get anywhere living the way I have been as my mother's keeper.

~ *Chapter 12* ~

I enter my old apartment and can see my mum is busying herself in the kitchen, cooking. The sight almost knocks me backwards. My mother…*cooking?!* The only thing my mother knows to cook are microwave meals, and even *that* can be tricky at times. Also standing in the kitchen is a very nicely dressed gentleman. *This must be her latest squeeze,* I think, rolling my eyes.

"Hi, sweetheart. This is John. John, Darla," my mother says, making the briefest of introductions.

"Hi, John. It is always lovely to meet a…*friend* of my mother's," I say, shaking John's hand. I notice he has well-manicured hands—no rough callouses or patches of skin anywhere—which says to me this man hasn't worked a hard day's graft in his whole life.

"Likewise. So, you're the infamous Darla I have heard so much about," John replies with a very nice posh English accent.

"I hope it's only good things my mother has been telling you."

"Of course."

"So, Mum, when did you decide to start using something other than the microwave?" I ask, really not wanting to make small talk or sitting here in awkward silence with *smooth* talking John.

"Well, as I was whisked off for a luxury break away last minute, I felt really bad, so I decided to research some easy recipes online and thought I'd take a crack at your favourite—mac 'n' cheese."

"You really shouldn't have troubled yourself," I mumble, as the overwhelming smell of burned cheese begins to fill the air.

"Nonsense! You're my little girl, and…where's Binks?" It suddenly clicks that I am, in fact, Bink-less.

"Actually, that's what I came to tell you. I've moved out."

My mother drops her spoon with sudden surprise, splashing thick, gloopy looking burnt cheese sauce out of the pan. "Moved out?" she shouts, alarmed.

"Yes. I am now living with a friend, which is where Binks is at the moment."

"How *marrrrvellous*. See, pookie? I *can* move in after all," John says, suddenly piping up, which earns him a glare from Mum. I briefly wonder where wonderful John resides, but as the thought enters my mind it quickly exits.

"Gosh, I have to head back and start getting ready for my shift at work. Sorry to miss out on the macaroni. It looks…yes, well…maybe next time we can cook together when I visit."

"Visit!" Mum cries, aghast. She is leaning against the tiny sideboard area for support as she swoons with my news that I won't be around so much.

"I think this is wonderful news –"

"With all due regards, John, I don't give a flying *fuck* what you think. Now sit down and shut up before I launch this macaroni at you," my mum growls, turning a darker shade of red.

Taking my mum's temper as my cue to leave, I beat a hasty retreat. Mum shouts a few more expletives once I'm outside. All things considered, my mum seemed to take the news rather well. John seems nice—in a wet, drippy sort of a way. It was comforting to me knowing my mum had company since I would no longer be living there. At least she won't be alone, so it was one less thing to worry about. There I go again, thinking like the parent. Yes, moving out is absolutely the best thing I can do for both of us.

My phone pings and I see a text from Dante. *Do you need a lift back to mine? How did things go with your mum?*

I rapidly respond with, *Yes, please to lift and Ok with my mum – coffee first?*

Dante sends me a wink face emoji before we decide on a rendezvous point. I find a small French style café and order a cappuccino while I wait for him. The temperature outside has dropped, so the inside heat brings welcome relief from the cold. The walls have faux flower baskets hanging from them, and on the far wall opposite me a mural has been painted of Paris on a summer's day with the Eiffel Tower in the centre. There is soothing French music playing through a speaker close to me, and the vibe is pleasant and mellow.

About twenty minutes later, Dante arrives, looking and smelling divine. Either I need to get a grip on my hormones, or things between us could get really messy...a *between the sheets* kind of messy and *blurring of lines* messy.

"I ordered a cappuccino. I hope that's ok, considering I left my purse back at yours."

"Oh, I'm sure I can stretch the pennies to buy you your coffee," Dante says, winking at me. He raises a hand to flag a waitress and orders us both ham and cheese croissants. I don't know about the cheese melting, but my heart sure is.

What is it with me and cheese today? I think humorously.

"How were things left with your mum?"

"Well, she has a new man."

"Good. That *is* good, right?"

"Mmm, hmm…I mean she was upset, of course, to hear of my sudden decision to move out, but this new guy, John, is apparently already moving in. It looks like things really have worked out for the best." I give a very watered-down version of the truth. I decided to leave out the fact that my mother actually threw the mother of all tantrums as I made my escape.

"Now, to change the subject…I have seen something that you might be interested in." Dante hands me the current copy of *Dance Now Magazine*. The magazine was opened to the page with a fill-in form.

"Holy crap! Pink Club…they are actually holding *open* auditions?!" I gasp, my eyes practically rolling out of my head as I glance over Pink Club's audition form.

"Yep, they sure are, and its open to anyone and everyone with professional dancing skills."

"I bet they have some really talented dancers applying from everywhere right now," I say flatly. Maybe in another life I could have considered myself good enough for an audition such as this, but with my financial and living situation being what they are, I don't think I could bare the rejection. It would be Busy Bee's all over again.

"I'm sure they do, and wouldn't it be *wonderful* to think another one could be applying soon?" Dante says with those *"come to bed"* eyes and big warm smile. I see what he is trying to do, but there's no way I could consider this—especially since the hot drink accident.

"Thank you for flattering me, but I doubt I'm anywhere close to good enough to go near Pink Club. I haven't got any serious professional dance experience outside of Busy Bee's."

"Excuse me! Pole dancing is a *very* professional dancing skill set that not many can muster," Dante states in a matter-of-fact tone.

I find myself unable to argue with him. I admit pole dancing *is* quite impressive. The amount of upper body strength we all need at Lucifer's Haven alone is above average for the everyday woman to muster if we are to be able to make the best most impressive moves. I guess I had never really given it much thought until now, as everything about the job had become robotic: a means to an end to making enough money to feed and house Mum and myself. It was a 'same shit, different day' scenario, but at least now it was only 'I' that I had to worry about—and Binks.

"Yes, but…I think the people they are looking for are more the types from good dancing schools or academies."

"The form does not stipulate exactly what requirements are necessary. Why don't you think on it?"

"Sorry, Dante, I'm just not up for putting myself through it. I'm just going to the loo before we leave. Thanks again for the coffee and for lunch."

"I'll settle the bill and meet you out by the car. I'm on the top level of the ACB carpark."

"See you in a bit."

~ *Chapter 13* ~

Dante sits behind the wheel of his black Bel-Air, tapping his fingers excitedly. The copy of *Dance Now Magazine* is next to him in the passenger seat, distracting him. Mulling it over, he decides on impulse to grab the magazine and hurriedly begins to fill in the necessary and relevant information, if only to bend the truth around her name.

First and Last Name: Prisma Faith

D.O.B: 1.1.1997

Age: 24

Address: Apt 12, Grayson St. EC1A 4AS

Contact number: 07779 215 715

Qualifications/Experience: Ballet Level 4 DDE Street
          Dance (Adv), Pole Dancing (Adv)

Email address: (Optional)   Eastgraffiti@Bunjee.com

All applications must be received by <u>*October the 15th*</u> *at the latest. Official audition dates will be sent out to everyone invited to come and audition for Pink Club. I look forward to meeting all of our chosen candidates soon.*
Kind Regards, Eva Godstone, Senior PR Manager for Pink Club

Taking a white envelope out of his glove box (Dante always has spares lying around for any necessary documents or letters that needed sending out to his dance students), he quickly and carefully tears out the form, putting it safely inside the envelope just as Darla is seen heading towards his car.

"Jump in. I just have to post these letters off for my students," Dante says, disguising the single letter by taking a big wad of blank envelopes with him.

"Ok, see you in a bit."

Pulse racing, it takes him a moment to steady his hand as he hurriedly writes the return address listed on the application form before he drops it into the post box. *Too late to back out now,* Dante thinks as he pockets the remaining envelopes before heading back to his car.

* * * * *

Watching Dante jog across the carpark to post his letters, I see the *Dance Now Magazine* on the dashboard and tell myself it's for the best that I get my head out of the clouds and forget about making it big in the world of dance. It's not meant to be. Time to grow up and be a realist. Dancing professionally is just not on the cards for me.

Sorry Nanna and Grandpa, I think just as Dante reappears. He enters his car bringing with him a most unwelcome cold blast of air.

We get to Dante's apartment, and Binks trots over to me, meowing excitedly. Giving my furry friend a cuddle, I then get busy fully unpacking my belongings. Glad to see no sign of Felicity anywhere. *Lying BITCH!* I think as I get re-acquainted with my space again.

"Knock, knock." I hear Dante's voice outside my door. "I've left you a mug of tea on the table. Make yourself at home. I have to get ready to teach this evening's class. When you leave, don't forget your key, which is also on the kitchen table."

I'm disappointed I can't make his weekday evening classes. "Cheers very much. See you later!" I shout through the door.

Once Dante leaves, I do a little celebratory dance around the living room space. I have never occupied such a large living area, and though it's probably small to people who live in very nice expensive houses or apartments, this—to me—is Heaven. I can actually twirl, for Heaven's sake! Twirl in the same room that has a dining table, sofa and television! The thought suddenly dawns on me that I'm yet to settle how much rent I'm to pay Dante to live here. I can understand why it must be a strain for just himself to afford this place. A two-bedroom apartment in a nicer area of London won't come cheap.

My shift at Chef No. 9 goes by quickly. Even Sarah noticed I have a bounce in my step. When it comes to closing for the night, we decide to go out for a few drinks now that our shift was over.

I ping a quick message to Dante to say that he is more than welcome to join us at The Old Docks karaoke bar once he finishes teaching for the night. He replied that he might see us there, and if not, he would leave the door unlocked for me to save me having to fumble for my key if I was to have one too many.

We head to Sarah's house first to freshen up, and she lets me borrow a bright green sparkly sequined dress. I do a mini spin in front of her floor-length mirror, admiring myself. We fix each other's hair and do a quick job of making up our faces before heading out.

"So, you're now living with your crush...permanently?" Sarah asks as we walk towards the bar. It's basically a local watering hole for our community and handily a stone's throw from Sarah's place.

"Well, yes, I am living there now, but I don't want to blur any boundaries."

"Pffft! Screw boundaries. I've seen Dante, and...well, if I was living where you are, I'd be all over *that* in a heartbeat," Sarah says with a smirk.

"Come on, *trouble*," I say, linking arms with Sarah as we head on into the bar.

The Old Docks is decked out to look similar to the underbelly of an old-fashioned pirate ship. The staff dress up as their own individualised pirate characters with braces full of funny pin badges. Fishing nets hang from the ceiling for decoration, and brightly coloured macaw parrots are dotted around the space alongside paintings and pictures of ships and sailors.

We find a booth towards a quieter area of the bar and flop down onto the purple leather upholstered seats.

"What can I get you two fine foxy ladies?" A strapping gentleman dressed in full pirate garb stands over us while holding the proverbial notepad and pen in hand.

"We'll have two Wet Sailors, two sting-ray steaks—medium rare— a Dragon salad to share, and...some Octo-fries please," Sarah orders for us. *The order translates into two alcoholic beverages of rum and Coke, two sirloin steaks, salad with chilies, and curly fries.*

"Are you sure you don't mind buying supper?"

"Relax. I got a windfall on the races last weekend and there is no one else I'd rather splurge on than my best friend and colleague," Sarah assures me. Her bright smile could light up any room. Sarah has fiery red hair, a load of freckles, and piercing green eyes. She also has two of the cutest dimples that show up every time she radiates light with that beautiful smile of hers.

"Come on, spill. What's the situation for real with you and this Dante guy?" she asks, really not letting me get away from giving her some information. I have no choice now that she has me cornered here in this booth.

The waiter, whose name—according to his driftwood nametag— is Jack (*how original,* I think), returns to our table with our drinks.

"Ok, but first I'd like to say cheers to us and cheers to life," I announce as we clunk tankards together before taking big swigs of our Wet Sailors.

"What is Dante like?"

"Speak of the devil," I nod in one direction where Sarah's eyes follow and almost roll out of her head.

Dante makes his way to our booth and plonks himself down next to me. He is still wearing his street dancing garb and looks just as gorgeous as ever.

"Well, hello there. You must be Dante. Darla has told me *so* much about you," Sarah coos, unapologetically drooling all over Dante.

The pair of them hit it off and are soon engaging in conversation to a rate I can barely keep up with. *Three is a crowd* comes to my mind as all I can do is watch them natter away. Our food finally arrives and there's an awkward moment when we realise Dante has no food.

69

"You can share mine," Sarah pipes up.

Well, that sorts out that problem then, I think, stabbing at a nice chunk of fresh lettuce without realising I've also stabbed a piece of chili…with seeds attached.

I ferociously chew on my mouthful as I watch the pair of them now outrageously flirting with each other. It takes mere seconds for me to realise that my mouth and throat are now aflame as my brain screams out signals, alerting me to the fact this is a Dragon salad to which I'm normally always careful about eating due to the chilies. *Stupid pride.*

Sarah and Dante happily continue to babble and I'm relieved when Sarah has to nip to the loo. My relief, however, is short lived when Dante also apparently has to nip to the loo. I sit in silence, pondering on the bizarre situation unfolding in front of me. I have never been able to speak with Dante the way Sarah now seems to be able to. The pair of them have barely said two words to me since he arrived, and I now seem to have been the unwitting component to, in fact, setting up my friend and colleague with my crush. And she knew he was my crush!

Angry thoughts swirl as I continually stab at my sting-ray steak and Octo-fries. The food is delicious, and Sarah is buying, but it still stings worse than the chili pepper in my mouth that she would even contemplate going there. Isn't there meant to be an unwritten code or something among friends that you don't pursue your friends crushes or exes? Clearly, no code exists here.

~ *Chapter 14* ~

Sarah seems to make the same error that I made with the Dragon salad, and it pauses her mouth just long enough for me to catch Dante's eye and for him to twig how ignored I have been this evening. I realise, though, that they really do have a spark here, and who am I to stand in the way of potential blossoming *true love*—even if it does mean my heart gets blasted into a million tiny pieces.

"Sorry, Darla. Hey, we should probably be making a move soon," Dante says, looking sympathetically at me.

Sarah regains her composure and makes a rapid writing motion with her hand to signal to Jack that she is ready to settle the bill. "Why don't you two stay a while longer. I'm happy to grab a cab home –"

"No, don't be silly. I'll drive us home. Sarah, it was lovely meeting you this evening, and thank you for the drinks and sharing your meal with me."

"Likewise, handsome."

The woman really is a menace, is all I can think. She really just has no idea—or just doesn't care about—how badly she's hurting my feelings right now.

We all stand together, and I can still feel the chemistry between these two annoyingly rolling off them in waves.

"Just going to nip to the loo. Won't be a moment," I say, leaving the pair looking still all google-eyed at each other. *I guess the chemistry I always imagined Dante and I would have really was just a fairy tale scenario in my own head,* I think while looking at my reflection in this moment of disappointment.

Once I clear my mind and put on my big girl pants, I begrudgingly give the pair my blessing under my breath. It they wish to hook up, I'll get over it. Dante is just a crush, after all, so I'm sure I can rise above this. And I can't be mad at Sarah, really; she's one of my closest friends. 'Hoes before Bro's' after all. Bonnie's mantra pops into my mind as I plaster a smile on my face and exit the ladies.

Dante is leaning against the wall outside of the toilet room, which startles me.

"God, you scared me," I say, holding hand to my chest. My heart now thunders a million beats an hour.

"I was beginning to think you'd fallen down the toilet. Sarah said to say goodbye and would see you at work," Dante tells me. He straightens up and beckons me to follow. "Come on, we both need a good night's kip. Everest Fitness has agreed to lease one of their dance studios on a regular basis. The council are going ahead with the closure of the community centre. I had to deliver the devastating news to my class this evening. What a shit day it's been. I'm glad we could do this," Dante continues.

I notice he really does look tired and a bit sad around the eyes. My heart softens towards Dante, and I realise Sarah was probably a much-

72

needed distraction from the stress he was currently under. He needed to laugh and relax, and she helped him to do that. *She did...not me.* Nope! I am not going to mope about this. I've made peace with this situation; time to move on.

"I'm so sorry to hear about the community centre, Dante. I'm happy to help with the move. I am relieved, though, that I can still dance in your classes. You had me worried there for a moment."

When we arrive back at Dante's apartment, it is the early hours of the morning. He heads straight for bed saying a brief *goodnight*.

I, however, am still quite wired. Deciding I can't chase sleep, I make myself a cup of tea. While the kettle boils, I notice some post on the side. Curiously, I go to have a nose, and it's then I see an opened letter that really does grab my attention—not because it's open, but because the name on the letter inside is not Dante's.

Sneakily, I push the post on the floor to make it look as if the letter would have just fallen on the floor conveniently...out of its envelope. The letter reads:

Dear Miss Faith,

Thank you for applying to audition for Pink Club. I am delighted to tell you that we have secured you a place for the 3rd of November at 10:15am.

The Address of the venue is: 35 Drake Lane Studios, London SE1 9PX

I very much look forward to seeing you then.

Warmest Wishes,

Eva Godstone, Senior PR Manager of Pink Club

I am frozen in place, yet my heart is beating wildly. *Ok...ok...let's just stay calm...this could easily be a dance student of Dante's. Yes, that's it. Phew, glad I worked out that dilemma. But who is Faith, then...why has the letter come here? Oh, my God. No…he wouldn't do that…would he? Shit! I am actually going to kill him!* I am unbelieving of Dante's clear insubordination of going behind my back and entering me into this auditioning process when I clearly told him I didn't want to apply for it.

My blood is singing with rage as I hear his bedroom door click open, and I hurry to put the post back the way I found it. Dante goes to the bathroom, and it is in this moment that a wicked plan enters my mind. I slip the opened envelope off the counter and carry it along with my tea into my bedroom. I smile to myself, imagining how he will undoubtedly be squirming later when recognition hits him that I now know what he has done behind my back.

The letter begins to draw my attention as it sits on top of my bedside table. My room is a far cry from the masculine tones of the main hub of the apartment. No, this room is all soft grey and pink tones. There is a very classy feminine touch to its design, and I feel right at home here.

Thoughts begin to pull my attention towards the letter, and before I know it, I'm re-reading it. They have accepted my application…but I'm not as experienced as the dancers who surely must be applying in their hundreds—if not thousands. What exactly did Dante do to get me my audition? And what's with the name? Oh…of course he would have wanted to hide my identity after the Chef No. 9 debacle. Now I wonder if they would have even considered me had my *real* name been put down, and what the hell will I do when I show up? Surely, they will recognise me immediately, call me out as a fraud, and have me either arrested or escorted out of the audition.

Fear swims in my head like a great white shark, systematically eating away at my dreams and what it could actually mean to dance for an establishment such as Pink Club. I eventually fall asleep, and what follows are troubled dreams of being naked and laughed at by Pink Club, then being chased by police dogs that catch up to me and tear at me with their sharp teeth, which jolts me awake. It takes me a full fifteen minutes, going by the illuminated clock on the wall, until I feel relaxed enough to be able to fall into a less troubled sleep.

~ *Chapter 15* ~

Eva sits in her office in quiet contemplation as relief washes over her. She has successfully narrowed down ten potential dancers through the arduous repetition of having to deny hundreds of others. Joshua calls to check in with her, and she feels very happy that she can now give him some positive news. It seems to please him, although she could never really gauge Joshua's mood at times, especially over the phone.

"Our big boss will be pleased to hear this," was his response for what was to be the briefest of conversations.

"Oh, don't mention it, *your majesty*. I've only aged about twenty years from all the stress while you go swanning off to Tuscany," Eva says to herself, but wanting to say this to Joshua. It is then she remembers to put the photograph of Mimi that sits on her desk back to the upright position now.

Joshua never mentions his sister anymore, and it's an unspoken rule that nobody else does either. He has been like a ghost presence at Pink Club since Mimi's murder, and with the big boss breathing down both their necks, it didn't help Eva when things went as wrong as they had. But, true to form—and proving she really *was* a super woman at PR—Eva had managed to sail their proverbial ship out of the storm and back into calmer waters.

* * * * *

The next morning when I awaken, I can already hear Dante pottering about in the kitchen. I open my bedroom just a smidgen and watch as he busies himself, putting bread in the toaster and setting out two mugs for tea. He is quite happily humming a tune to himself, but when he turns to pick up the mail on the sideboard and starts flicking through it, he pauses, and a moment of panic crosses his face. He must realise the letter for 'Prisma Faith' is now nowhere to be seen. I stifle a cheeky giggle, watching him.

Dante is soon feverishly checking on the floor, in and under cupboards, and flitting around the living room space, checking the coffee table while looking very concerned. I wait until he's almost on the verge of having what looks like a panic attack before lazily making my entrance, yawning as if totally oblivious to the hilarious scene that just unfolded in front of me. The letter is burning a hole in my pyjama dressing gown pocket.

"Good morning, Dante. Did you sleep well?" I ask, stretching my arms up over my head.

"Erm, yes, thank you. Now where is it?!" he mutters, more to himself than to me.

"Where's what? Have you lost something?"

"Just some mail. I could have sworn I left it right here…ah, maybe I took it to my bedroom. Be right back." He quickly dashes off in the direction of his bedroom, and while he is out of sight, I take the letter out of its envelope and then tuck the empty envelope between a small house plant on the sideboard and the wall.

"This wouldn't be it by any chance, would it?" I call out to Dante, who then comes galloping back into the kitchen. He quickly whips the white envelope out of my hand once his eyes see it.

Opening the envelope, Dante despairs that it is empty. He literally picks it up, holds it above his head and shakes it, as if wishing by some miracle that the letter will materialise. He then collapses onto a bar stool next to me, looking exhausted.

The toast pops, so I leave Dante to wonder more on his puzzlement of the missing letter as I pour the tea and butter the toast. I finally decide he's sweated enough, so as I place his cup of tea and toast in front of him, I also slip the letter forward.

Dante raises his head off the countertop and then turns to look at me very sheepishly. "I think…we need to talk," he says.

"Yes! I think we do!" I reply in my best strict headmistress tone of voice.

~ *Chapter 16* ~

"I can explain –"

"No need. Look, I have had most of the night to think about this, and although I was shocked to see that you went behind my back on this –"

"And I am wholeheartedly sorry about that –"

"Let me finish."

"Sorry, by all means, please carry on."

"Right. So, as I was saying, I've thought on this for most of the night, and so long as you call up this PR woman, Eva Godstone, and let her know the name on the form was wrong and give my real name, then I will go for the audition."

"That's fantastic, Darla. Well done for making such a gutsy decision. Of course I will straighten out the name issue right away. I'm sorry again for applying for you on the sly. I was going to tell you, but I didn't get round to revealing what I'd done before…you found out. It really was done with the best of intentions," Dante says, looking at me with a sorrowful expression. I decide to let him off the hook.

"In a way, I'm glad that you put me forward. Once I got over my fear and surprise at seeing this letter, and I could mull it over, I thought, why wouldn't I apply? I would be crazy not to go for this once in a lifetime experience." I feel more at ease with my decision to go for the audition, if not just for the amazing experience and to be able to say, "I was good enough to audition for an establishment such as Pink Club."

"Now there's the confident Darla I know. I'm glad to see she has her spark back."

"Also, my grandparents would have eagerly persuaded me to do the audition, had my grandfather still been alive—God rest his soul— and if my gran still had all her marbles. Speaking of which—I have arranged to see my gran today. Would you mind giving me a lift?"

"They would be so proud of you. I know I am, as both your friend and teacher. And, yes, I will take you to see your gran."

I hug Dante and thank him for helping to push me outside of my comfort zone and take this chance. It is a hug just between friends, and the sense of awkwardness from my previous 'crush' type feeling has left me, as I realise he really does like Sarah. Since the evening they met at The Old Docks karaoke bar, I am sure they have been in phone contact. I can't be mad; they are both my friends and I'm happy for them…even if still a little jealous.

"Right, well, I'd best call Eva and let her know I made an error on the application form. Would you mind at all if I mention to them that I'm your dance teacher? It just means that if you do well, and heck, even get offered a position at the club, it would look really good for me."

"Well, it is the truth—you are my dance teacher—and the only reason I'm doing this is because of your encouragement and belief that I'm good enough for this opportunity, so please feel free. On that note, I'm going to have a shower."

"I'd best get ready myself. See you in a bit. "

We arrive at Safe Haven Forever Home, which is a lower budget home for the elderly. It is all Mum could afford from the money left over from what Grandad left, and to ensure Gran got great care.

The home is a small old Victorian house that was refurbished with an extra wing added before it was opened officially in 1985 as an elderly care home. The staff have always been very friendly, and Gran has always appeared well looked after, which is one less thing to stress about.

Dante decides he will wait in the car for me to give me some privacy. As I head inside with the flowers I bought for her, I notice the sky is clear and blue and there is a fresh chill in the air. Even though it's cold, it still feels nice to have some sun on my face.

Walking in towards reception, I notice the log burner is on, and the sweet woody aroma gives a heady, homely feel. A woman whose name tag reads *Jane* sits at reception. She just finishes speaking to someone over the phone and then helps book me in. I am given my visitor pass, and Jane then offers to take the flowers and put them in a vase and into Gran's room. I am told that Gran is in the lounge, being read to by a new member of staff named Martha.

Entering the lounge area, I see that my grandmother, who is sitting next to a fireplace, is indeed being read to by a young woman who must be Martha. The lounge is cosy and there are a pair of gentlemen playing chess. Someone else is painting and a few more residents are watching a movie.

"Hi, Gran," I say. As she turns to me, I already know she is completely unaware of who I am.

"Hello, there. My name is Martha." A dark-haired young woman, wearing a bright red cardigan over her white blouse, introduces herself while shaking my hand. She comes across very warm and friendly, and it pleases me she is taking the time to read to my grandmother.

"I will give you two some privacy," Martha says, excusing herself.

"It was lovely to meet you," I say as she goes to tend to some of the other residents. I then turn to Gran. "Hello, Gran. It's me, Darla." I kneel in front of her and hold her fragile, gnarled hands.

"Have you come to give me my bath?" she asks.

I can't help but smile at her muddle-lindeness. Picking up the book Martha left on the chair, I decide to continue the story. The book is called "Mischief is Magical" and the back of the book says it is about a cat named Mischief who gets up to all sorts of magical and mischievous adventures.

As I continue from where Martha left off, I hear a classical piece of music beginning to play through one of the speakers on the wall that has been serenely serenading everyone. I recognise the piece immediately—it is six consolations in D flat major. I would practice my ballet to this piece over and over again as a child, and my grandmother would praise and clap as I twirled around hers and grandad's living room in my pink ballet garb.

"My granddaughter, Darla, dances ballet, you know. I watch her practice to this very piece of music."

My jaw almost hits the floor as the words leave my grandmother's mouth. Elation and raw emotion flood my body as she seems to recall the memory. "Gran, it's me…Darla," I whisper, clasping her hands once more.

"Darla…it is you? My, how you've grown."

"I'm going to audition for a big competition. I'm going to change my life; I really am."

The music fades and another track takes its place.

"That's nice dear. Is it lasagne or macaroni tonight?"

I see the faint glimmer of recognition dissolve from my gran's eyes, as the vacant expression returns, and I lose her once more to this thief of a disease robbing me of her light again.

"Would you like me to replay the track? It might help her to interact with you better," Martha says, approaching us. She must have noticed our brief moment of intimacy where—for just a few seconds—we were grandmother and granddaughter again.

I thank Martha for the offer, but I don't want this moment in time and memory ruined by trying to force her to remember more.

"Goodbye, Gran. I love you. Oh, and the flowers in your room are from me."

Martha takes the book from my hands and places a reassuring hand on my shoulder. "I will take good care of her," she assures me.

Back in Dante's car, I breathe a sigh of relief and then proceed to burst into a fresh bout of tears. Dante wonders what on earth is the matter with me before I am able to take a moment to compose myself and tell him of the amazing moment I had just shared inside the home with my grandmother.

~ *Chapter 17* ~

"Come on, there's one place I know where we can go that will cheer you up," Dante announces as he drives away from the home.

"Really? Where is that?"

"The dance studio. I have blocked out an hour at Everest Fitness for us to begin to put your audition choreography together."

"She was just...*herself* for the briefest of moments and then gone again," I say, not hearing Dante. I was too wrapped up in the grief of how dementia has robbed me of my grandmother before she would ever know I made a success of my dancing.

"Come on, she wouldn't want to see you upset," Dante says, giving my hand a gentle squeeze before placing it back to the steering wheel.

The sensation of Dante's hand having been on top of mine breaks me out of my sad reverie—enough to start talking about other things dance related.

"I'm looking forward to working with you on my choreography."

"Me too, but first...food! I'm starving. Shall we pop to the drive-thru on our way there?" Dante asks. He is grinning at me wickedly, as he already knows that the mere mention of comfort food will be too hard for me to turn down.

Once we have our burgers and fries, Dante parks his car so we can eat. I feel better once I have some fuel in my stomach and can then reflect on the amazing trip to see my gran with fresh eyes. The sadness has ebbed away and now I can just view today as a happy memory. I can't stop or cure her dementia, but of all the things she *does* recall from memory is me, and that thought makes me feel happier.

We finally arrive at Everest Fitness. The building is like a big brick cube with tall windows all around it so that people can see in. It is just two floors—the exercise studios are on the first floor and the gym is on the second floor. The place is always busy, and pedestrians or drivers going past can see exactly what type of a business Everest Fitness is. The windows were a great advertisement idea.

Once we settle inside the studio, Dante uses a remote control to put the blinds down. That is the other nice feature about the fitness centre: if dancers want privacy—for, example, pole dancing practice— they can put the blinds down. The far wall is classically lined with floor to ceiling length mirrors, and a bar runs alongside the mirrors for ballet dancers to use for stretching and balancing. This place feels so much like home to me, having danced for so many hours in the Busy Bee's dance studio.

We do a lengthy gentle warm up, having only just eaten, but are soon in full swing. Dante chooses the music track "Chase the Night Away," saying it will conjure up feelings of emotion for the judges and that the theme of my dance should be life as it is right now for me. For a waitress working long hours, but with a big dream of dancing, that seems insurmountable with all the financial blocks. I love this idea and agree that tugging at the judges' heartstrings could be the ace card I need up my sleeve to give me a real fighting chance. After all, my grandfather used to say that people never remember what you say in life to them, but they always remember how you made them feel. I want to make the judges remember how I make them feel through my dance, even if they don't remember much about the routine itself.

We now have some skeletal ideas, and as the time runs out for our usage of the studio—signalled by the next wave of people waiting to use the space, standing outside—we decide to head back to the apartment to brainstorm further.

My costume is to be a sexier version of what I wear at Chef No. 9, complete with sheer, skin-coloured tights, black hot pants, a white short sleeved shirt, and black apron. My prop for the dance will be a single black chair.

I also call both Chef No. 9 and Lucifer's Haven to take two weeks holiday effective immediately. It is short notice, but before anyone has booked Christmas holiday, so to my delight, I'm granted the time off without much fuss.

The next two weeks pass in a bit of a blur, and as I get closer to my audition date, my nervousness increases. Sarah has been coming along, not just to spend time with Dante but to also give me moral support. She loves my routine and has helped get my costume together, as she is a secret seamstress ninja that not many people know about. I lost count of the many times I've needed a button sewn back on something or a zipper fixed on a bag of mine or pair of trousers.

Dante and Sarah are not 'officially' an item yet, but they have been spending lots of time together when I'm not practicing my dance routine with him. Seeing how happy they are together makes it easier to tolerate, though at times my inner green monster would love nothing more dearly than to push them both into the Thames— especially on the nights when I am thankful to have my headphones on hand as my best friend and crush get busy between the sheets.

It's now the night before my audition and my nerves are in full swing. Sarah has kindly swapped a shift with someone at Chef No. 9 so she can be at Dante's place bright and early to help fix my hair and make sure my costume is nothing but pukka ready for my audition.

"I guess I had better make a move, and whatever happens tomorrow, I insist that we go out and celebrate," Sarah says, her eyes bright.

Clearly, she's full of all those 'love' hormones, I think bitterly.

"Sounds good; let me see you out," Dante says, walking Sarah to his door. I busy myself with Binks, playing with one of his cat toys on a string that has him scrabbling about.

"See you tomorrow, Darla," Sarah calls, waving animatedly to me before ducking out into the corridor with Dante. I smile, and then once I see they are out of sight, stick my finger up at the door. My jealous green monster appears, still smiting from the blow I've been dealt about my crush and best friend getting things together.

Feeling tired and stuffed from the pizza we all enjoyed while watching some cheesy romcom on the TV, I resign myself to bed. Dante and I only did a light run through today of my routine. He said that I needed to conserve my energy for the big day ahead and make sure my feet were in perfect working order, which they were.

It was an alien concept for me to do hardly anything dance

rehearsal related the day before a big audition. When I was at Busy Bee's, Marie made us dance until sometimes my feet did actually bleed. She didn't care if we were in pain on competition day; we were told to suck it up and get on with it. Everyone—for fear of losing their place at her dance school—did just that. Of course, competition wins give her lots of money and publicity, which must be the driving force behind her brutal teaching regime.

I will, however, never forgive her for denying me the free scholarship she offers her other students simply because of my living situation. Once my grandfather passed away and she found out I couldn't afford the fees—although I applied for the scholarship—it apparently had already been snapped up…by my replacement. My trust in teachers met with shaky ground after that, until one afternoon Dante had seen me thrashing it out in the soon-to-be-demolished community centre dance studio. Interested, he stood and watched me until I was spent.

Introducing himself as a street dance teacher, and handing me one of his advertising leaflets, I mulled over taking my dance skills in a newer direction, and together we began to blend ballet and street dance together. Dante also was a male pole dancer and taught me how to gradually learn and build my skills around this before I was employed as a dancer for Lucifer's Haven. I asked him why he never competed, and he said he liked the simplicity teaching dance brought with it and got far more enjoyment watching some of his students do really well.

Reminiscing on how and why we became friends my heart softens again towards his new romantic venture with Sarah. *I will get over it one day…I'm sure I will…*

~ *Chapter 18* ~

Sarah arrives at 6:30 a.m. Her and Dante left me to sleep a bit longer until rousing me at 7:30. "Morning, sleepy head. I've made you some nice fresh pancakes garnished with strawberries—something nice and light before your big debut on that Pink Club auditioning stage," Sarah says, melting my heart.

Ok, yes, I can absolutely forgive you for hooking up with crush, I think, as it's in this very moment I realise that friends like Sarah are rare and few.

"Where is Dante?" I ask quizzically.

"He's in the shower. How are you feeling about this morning's audition?"

"Obviously nervous, but I don't think I will know exactly how I feel until it's all over," I tell her truthfully. I take a bite of pancake, noticing how deliciously light and fluffy it feels in my mouth, and it takes the edge off my morning dance nerves for a mere moment.

"Considering the list of applicants is so small, I'd say you have a real fighting chance," Sarah responds in a matter-of-fact tone, which stops me eating.

"Sorry…you know this *how?*"

"Oh, oops! Dante had said to keep that detail back from you. Ah, well, cat's out of the bag now, so brace yourself. You're one of ten people that have been invited to go through the auditioning process."

Here I was thinking there would be long lines of people going to audition, meaning I could just break myself back into dancing under pressure gradually again. But now this bombshell just landed and my brain didn't quite know how to process what Sarah has said.

"I just have to pop to the loo. Back in a mo," I say, swiftly getting up and fast walking to the bathroom in my room. "Don't be sick…deep breaths…need the energy. Come on, now…deep breath in two…three…four, and out two…three…four. See? Piece of cake," I assure myself as the nausea ebbs away.

I hear Dante exit the bathroom and begin a conversation with Sarah. Once I have my head cleared, I head back out. My pancakes sit unfinished. Since dancing on a partially empty stomach will do me no good, I chew them down with my now very dry mouth from nerves.

"There she is—the star of the day!" Dante exclaims with a big goofy grin. I could gladly slap the grin right off his face from keeping such a crucial detail away from me.

I ignore Dante and finish my breakfast, thanking Sarah for taking the time and effort to do something so nice for me.

"Right. You had better start getting dressed into your costume. I'll go and warm the car up and then it's all systems go," Dante spouts chipperly, unaware of the anxiety now coursing through my veins.

As he walks past me, I get a whiff of his heady aftershave and know that it is literally impossible for me to stay mad with the flurry of lust hormones now injected into my psyche.

Dammit, still crushing after crush! I think, annoyed at my body and its hormones.

"Ready?" Sarah appears with my costume in hand.

"About as ready as I'll ever be. Come on, the sooner I get this over with and they all tell me how crap I am at dancing, the sooner I can drown my sorrows with you and Dante back at The Old Docks and get back to *normal* life."

"If it's any consolation, I really *do* believe you're in with a winning chance. When you've taught me some of the basic steps in dancing on the evenings we lock up together, I can see that you really are very talented, Darla. Don't sell yourself short," Sarah says, giving me a hug.

"Aww, thank you. Seriously, though, drinks are on me once this ordeal is over." I head back to my bedroom to get dressed.

* * * * *

It is day two at the auditioning venue. The first five candidates that turned up to audition the day before yielded no hope.

"I can't believe we are struggling so badly to find dancers who can actually dance. You'd have thought people would have been lining up outside the doors for this opportunity!" Eva cries, as Octavia nibbles on a chocolate digestive.

"It's just the wrong time of year to be advertising; too close to Christmas when everyone has their contracts and jobs sorted for shows before the spring," Octavia shrugs.

"And where is that bloody Mr. Whitty?" Eva almost shouts as she waits impatiently for the third judge on their panel to show up.

91

"Speak of the devil," Octavia points.

A man in a tweed suit and briefcase walks in across the hall to the small white pop-up table Eva and Octavia are sitting at. Mr. Whitty is a performing arts teacher for a local college who was able to give up some free time for a small fee to help with the judging process, per Octavia's request.

"Good morning, ladies. Let's hope today gets you a better result for your dance club than yesterday. It was certainly entertaining, given the very fact that I think I saw some of the worst examples of dancing in my twenty-year-long career in this profession," Mr. Whitty grumbles, which gets right under Eva's skin.

Eva swallows her retort and gets ready to call forward the first candidate of the day.

The morning begins just as uneventfully as yesterday. The first two candidates were flat out crap and untalented, clearly just looking to waste everyone's time, including their own. By the time it comes to calling their last candidate, Eva, Octavia and Mr. Whitty look as if they have all but lost the will to live.

"Darla Pebble...*Darla*...does that name ring any bells for you, V?" Eva asks, repeating the name Darla Pebble over and over again in her head. It was like a tune to a song you can't remember the title to, but it sits on the tip of one's tongue.

"No, should it?" she replies, opening a fresh bottle of water before taking a long swig from it.

"Right...well, in that case, I'm off to the loo and hopefully I'll be back when it's all over," Eva announces. She stands up and excuses herself while still pondering on the name.

Reaching the toilets and taking a pew, Eva proceeds to scroll through the news feed on her mobile. It is then that she skims past a name that looks almost the same as Darla Pebble. Rapidly scrolling back again, there it is: the tabloid newspaper article, complete with graphic photo of the young woman named Darla Pebble on her knees. The title of the article says:

Waitress cum (pun intended) 'blow job girl' helps wealthy Mr. Glass get his rocks off in a crowded restaurant just hours after the announcement of Pink Clubs' lead dancer's death.

"Shit!" Eva exclaims. She jumps from her pew rapidly and drops her phone in the process. The phone slips under the toilet cubicle door and is sent sprawling across the floor. She fiddles with the lock on the door, and it soon dawns on Eva that she has become well and truly stuck. A laminated piece of paper falls from the other side of the door, half slipping under it, and she picks it up, alarmed to see it reads **Out of Order.** Eva had missed the notice completely as she had been too busy with her head buried in her phone. Now she was without phone or any hope of escaping her toilet cell until someone came looking for her.

"Bloody Darla Pebble!" Eva shouts to the ceiling.

~ *Chapter 19* ~

"Calling to the stage now, Miss Darla Pebble!" A man's voice reverberates loudly out of the small microphone sitting in front of him as I step out onto the big brightly lit staging area.

"Good morning, Miss Pebble. My name is Reginald Whitty and this here is Octavia Perez. Eva should be along shortly, but you may begin while we wait for her," Mr. Whitty greets.

"Tell us a bit about yourself," Octavia Perez calls out before I begin. I recognise her instantly from *Dance Now Magazine* articles and occasional TV appearances. Octavia has beautiful mocha coloured skin, piercing green eyes, and long black braids with wisps of electric blue woven in. The gentleman, I notice, looks most out of place here and more like he should be sitting as a headmaster in a school somewhere.

My heart is thundering away as I tell the judges my name and how much I love to dance. Mr. Whitty takes his glasses off his face and squeezes the bridge of his nose on hearing this. I imagine it must have been something said by all the other candidates. (All the other candidates—who am I kidding, there are only ten of us.) They look just as keen for this to be over as I do, so I won't disappoint them by continuing to waffle on about myself.

"Take it away, Darla," Octavia instructs.

The lights dim and I take the briefest moment to compose myself before peering at the backstage curtain and giving Dante the thumbs up signal to start the music. Sarah gives me two thumbs up in return and I respond with a swift smile.

My black chair prop is in the centre of the stage. Once the spotlight and music come to life around me, I begin my routine and quickly lose myself to the tempo and rhythm of the song "Chase the Night Away" by Keane. I pour all my emotion and frustration that I can muster into the story I'm hoping to get across to the judges. Thoughts of my grandparents surface, and I use that feeling of emotional grief to express further the vast range of my dance skills, having combined street dance and ballet into my routine.

As the music comes to a close, and I wrap my routine up, the spotlight turns off and the main lights come back up again. Octavia and Reginald get out of their seats to give me a standing ovation. I bring my hands to my face, stunned to see such a positive reaction.

"Wow—oh, wow! Girl, you have got some *mooooves,*" Octavia Perez calls out in her rich Latino accent.

"Yes, I also must admit that the show of dance skills you just displayed is vastly above what we've seen here throughout this audition," Reginald adds.

Just as I'm lapping up all the compliments, a woman with pink hair comes bounding across to the fore, and she looks about as pink-faced as her hair. I recognise immediately that this is Eva Godstone. I feel sad that she missed my routine, but my disappointment is only short lived.

"Ok, if you're really so good, *Darla Pebble,* then please repeat the routine. I'm sorry I am late. I got…stuck…on an urgent call."

"This is Eva Godstone –"

"She knows who I am, Reginald. Isn't that right, *Blow Job Girl?*"

As soon as Eva says the words 'Blow Job Girl' I notice that Reginald spits his mouthful of tea out, Octavia's jaw drops open, and I freeze like a deer in headlights. I cannot believe what Eva has just said in front of the other two judges. My head begins to swim from the shock and embarrassment.

"I'm sorry…this was a mistake," is all I manage to say before running off the stage, completely mortified and wanting the ground to swallow me up.

"That's right, time waster! Go back to waiting tables. Honestly, talk about adding insult to injury! First, she almost scalds Joshua and I, then thinks she can muscle her way into this audition. No, scrap her from the list as well," Eva sneers, causing both Octavia and Reginald to look at her, aghast.

"Now hang on just one second!" I hear Reginald start in my defence.

But the damage is done. My worst fear has come true. I have been embarrassed, rejected and humiliated.

I see Dante storm out with a murderous expression on his face as I pass him, running in the opposite direction, imagining he's to give Eva Godstone a mouthful. Sarah tries to run after me but must have given up because when I stop for breath, she is nowhere to be seen.

I want to be alone, and it looks as if my wish is granted, as I'm now lost in this huge warehouse location, unsure of where I am or where to get back to where I had just come from, and I haven't got my mobile phone on me. I just have to sit and wait until I can be found. Under normal circumstances (not that I'd ever find myself in such a location under normal circumstances), I'd probably be shitting myself to be lost. But as I bask in how quiet the corridor is, it gives me a moment to collect my thoughts and also to calm down. I sit down, resting my head on my knees, and tears begin streaming down my face.

"Darla, there you are!" Sarah is jogging over to me.

"I got lost…can we go home now?" I wipe tears away from my red-rimmed eyes.

Sarah hands me a tissue and helps me to stand, putting a friendly arm around me. "Come on, let's find Dante and sort this out," Sarah says determinedly.

I am not so sure there is anything to sort out. Eva had just made her thoughts very clear of what she thought of me. I still can't form words properly, as the shock of what has just happened still reverberates inside my mind.

Thankfully, Sarah's sense of direction is better than mine, and we both manage to make it back to the main staging area. Sarah's mobile pings and it's Dante, so she lets him know where we are. A short while later, Dante reappears with Octavia Perez and Reginald Whitty, though Eva Godstone is now nowhere to be seen.

"Darla, I am so sorry for Eva's outburst; it is most out of character for her, and I know personally that she has been under an incredible amount of stress since Bella's death," Octavia explains. I do feel she is being sincere, but it does nothing to soften the blow that has just been dealt to me.

"Yes, well, stress or not, I found it to be deeply embarrassing and can't begin to imagine how poor Darla must be feeling," Reginald jumps in before I can reply.

"What is going to happen now? Shall I just go?" I ask, dreading the answer but also wanting to get the hell away from here.

"I will tell you what is going to happen. Eva will be giving you a full apology, and as this has turned into a bit of an emergency, I called my boss, Joshua. As luck would have it, he arrived back in the U.K. last night. Under his instruction, he has sent Eva home and is instead coming here to watch you audition. It would have to be Eva or Joshua who had the final say, so unfortunately you will need to dance again," Octavia tells me, delivering news that was the furthest thing possible to being music to my ears.

"You mean Joshua—as in *THE* Joshua Glass—will be watching my audition?" I was becoming woollier headed by the second.

This morning had not panned out as I'd hoped. My plan to have been fairly merry by now—drowning my sorrows down at The Old Docks with Dante and Sarah while wallowing from the negative commentary received from the judging panel—had been interfered with by fate. Now here I am about to audition (again) in front of none other than *THE* Joshua Glass. My poor brain feels fried.

"The very same. Ah, I've just been notified by his driver that he has arrived," Reginald Whitty informs us, which all but makes my legs buckle.

This is going from the sublime to the ridiculous! What a shit-show! Do I really

98

want to subject myself to yet more rejection? My mind now races at a million miles an hour along with my now thundering heartbeat.

"Are you alright, Darla? You've gone an awfully pale shade of white," Sarah asks, concerned.

"I'm…I'm…"

"Here, have two of these chocolate digestives," Octavia offers, handing me the biscuits. I thankfully start to munch on them, but my mouth is dry, so it makes chewing and swallowing quite difficult.

"Darla, can I borrow you for a moment?" Dante asks, leading me to one side.

"What is it now?" I am alarmed, as my normal thought processes are not functioning properly at all.

"Chill out! From what Octavia and the serious-looking dude have said, you pretty much have the job!"

"I *do?!*"

"Yes. Running through the dance again is just a formality. Now, come on, you can do this. Go to the toilets and splash some cold water on your face. Joshua will be here presently." Dante urges me to get my shit together. The smell of his aftershave awakens a weak sense of lust within me, which is all I need to come softly back down to earth ready to face the challenge head on.

"I'm fine, really. I'm ready," I insist, giving off a big sigh.

Sure enough, Joshua Glass appears with his bodyguard who I vaguely remember from the morning of the accident at Chef No. 9.

"Ah, Miss Pebble, is it?"

"Y-yes," I stammer, feeling as if I should curtsey or something. The familiar feeling of red flushes my cheeks at seeing him in the flesh again.

"So sorry about my colleague's outburst, but if we could crack on that would be grand. I have a busy day ahead, as I'm sure we all do. When you're ready, you may begin." Joshua commands the space effortlessly with how he conducts himself in such a professional manner, which gives me a bolstered sense of confidence as, once more, I take up position centre stage and begin my dance routine (again).

~ *Chapter 20* ~

I finish my dance and await with bated breath to see what the judges have to say *this* time around. Joshua is animatedly chatting to Reginald and Octavia, leaving me just standing in awkward silence on stage. They are all nodding in unison before Joshua gets up to briskly walk out along with his bodyguard, completely ignoring me this time (*rude*).

Reginald and Octavia carry on the conversation until I am called down off the stage to the judges' desk. I glance back towards where Dante and Sarah stand behind the stage curtain, and they encourage me with smiles and nods.

Bracing myself, I walk to where Reginald and Octavia sit. Reginald stands, shaking Octavia's hand before turning to me to shake my hand and telling me it was a pleasure for him to watch me dance this morning. Then he wishes me "the very best of luck with my dancing future" before walking off, briefcase in hand.

"Right, well, it looks like…you got the job!" Octavia announces, flashing me a huge perfectly symmetrical toothy grin.

"Wow! Seriously? I really got the job? I'm going to be –"

"That's right, you're about to become our new leading dance lady."

I all but faint from hearing Octavia say this. After so many years of wanting a shot at the big time as a dancer, right here, right now it feels as if a magic genie is granting me my one true lifelong wish.

"What happens now?" My voice is a bit shaken from all the excitement of the moment.

"I imagine you will be promptly invited down to Pink Club, more than likely tomorrow, so you may wish to clear your schedule. Eva will give you more on the details, as I am just their dance choreographer. On a more serious note, though, very well done. That was some fantastic dancing you demonstrated up there today, and you should feel very proud. Big pat on the back for you."

"So glad to hear our girl here got the job!" Dante says, placing a hand on my shoulder. My heart thunders away again.

"It was a real pleasure getting to watch Darla showcase her dancing skills here today. Good to see you again, Dante. Your looking…well," Octavia says as her cheeks tinge the slightest shade of red. Then I remember that he had told me he has history with the Pink Club troupe and Octavia.

"Cheers, as do you. Right, well, I guess that's it for today then. Do you have to dash off or would you like to join us to celebrate?"

"I…really should be off. Lots to plan for Darla's big arrival now," Octavia explains, winking at me.

I blush slightly before we all head out of the building. As we reach the exit, reporters—who must have followed Joshua Glass here—are loitering outside, so as we leave, there are flashes from cameras and a mob swiftly gathers to shove microphones at us.

My heart momentarily leaps into my mouth, but once they realise we are seemingly nothing special, they shrink back. I figure they think we are some sort of event staff because, as quickly as they approach us, they back off, taking up their original spaces near to the doors.

Once we are out of earshot of the press, Octavia mentions that I will get used to press attention and that everyone at Pink Club has regular training on how to be safe at functions and events where there will be a heavy media presence. She then says a swift goodbye to us as she heads to her car.

Dante, Sarah and I all decide that it is too early to get sozzled—especially as Sarah is due to be at work at Chef No. 9 soon—so we opt instead to have some celebratory nibbles and coffee at Angel Cake.

"Well, I would just like to say cheers to you, Darla. Very well done for stepping up, facing your fears, and absolutely smashing that audition," Dante declares, as we carefully chink coffee mugs together.

"I am gonna miss you loads at Chef No. 9, but I'm really pleased to see you making a go of things with your dancing. Just don't forget who your friends are when you're rich and famous," Sarah teases, winking at me.

"Thank you so much for supporting me today for what was a *craaaazy* morning. Honestly, I couldn't have got through today without you two, and I promise you –"

"Careful, now, don't make promises you can't keep," Dante interrupts playfully.

I jab him in the arm just as playfully and continue. "As I was saying, I *promise* both of you that I will still be in regular contact, and although we may see less of each other, we will still get together and have fun."

103

I know that chance will be a fine thing once my new career path takes off, and this thought suddenly saddens me immensely.

"To great friends," Sarah proclaims, and we all cheer again.

Sarah and Dante share a chaste kiss in front of me and, for the first time, I realise I'm not jealous anymore. They just seem so right for each other, which maybe has something to do with it.

* * * * *

Eva sits in Joshua's office, looking ahead at the oversized, blown-up black and white photo of Mimi that hangs behind his black Obsidian desk. Unlike Eva's office, which has warm tones of creams and coffee colours to it, Joshua's office has harsh metallic tones with black and white accents.

"Ok, so here is the contract for Darla. I take it I can trust you to deliver that to her without causing further embarrassment to me or our business here?" Joshua challenges coolly.

Eva nods her head. "I really am sorry Joshua. I feel terrible –"

"No less terrible than you made that poor woman feel," he interjects curtly.

Eva makes a throat clearing sound before carrying on. "What time would you like me to bring her here tomorrow to begin learning the ropes?" Eva asks, ignoring Joshua's previous comment.

"Let's give her a lie in, so say 10:30 a.m."

"Very good. Will you be here –"

"I will be busy with other engagements."

"Do you need me to inform Stella that crisis has been averted regarding the spring gala, as we now have a new lead dance act on the books, or would you like to do that yourself?" Eva asks smugly, knowing the mention of the name 'Stella' will undoubtedly irk him.

"I'm sure you can handle that," Joshua responds as he stands, his back turned to Eva. He then slips his suit jacket on before proceeding to march straight past her and out of his office.

Eva's face drops, now knowing she will have to speak to their big boss, Stella Almasi, a blood thirsty aristocrat. Before her untimely death, Mimi had confided to Eva that Joshua and Stella had a romantic fling, but it all blew up in his face once he realised she was married to a very wealthy Arab yacht salesman. If that wasn't bad enough, Stella had also fraudulently put Joshua's name down as guarantor so she could side swipe him and Mimi of their nightclub business venture. If they dared team up against her, she would pull the funds, leaving them bankrupt.

When Eva had pressed Mimi to find out how this all came about, Mimi explained that Stella caught wind of this new nightclub idea along the grapevine from her high society friends on social media the same time Joshua and Mimi were actively looking for beneficiaries. She then plotted to worm her way in by using Joshua as a 'boy toy' just to steal his and Mimi's nightclub idea. As they didn't have the funding, Stella came in almost like a fairy godmother and seemed to make all their financial worries disappear.

If what Mimi had told Eva was to be believed, Stella had wrangled things so well that she made sure she was not only beneficiary but also owner of Pink Club, having ownership of all the rights. However, she wanted to stay off scene, in the background, using Joshua and Mimi as the face of the company because they gave a much *'prettier'* image for the younger generation than she could, as she was pushing forty. Joshua tried to find some way out of the mess, but she had tied him in so many legal knots and red tape, he was well and truly stuck.

Eva never confirmed this with Joshua, as it was told to her in the strictest of confidence when she came on board to work for Pink Club as their senior PR manager.

With Joshua gone, and now that she knew what his wishes were, Eva begrudgingly picked up the phone and dialled in Stella Almasi's number while closing her eyes and taking a deep breath, just imagining Stella sitting on the toilet to help ease her nervousness around the ensuing conversation.

~ *Chapter 21* ~

"Hi, only me," I chirp, entering my mum (and now John's) apartment. I'd decided to drop round there after my audition was over and clear the air with my mum, bringing flowers for her.

John takes the flowers from me and sets them in a small vase on the coffee table. They seem to have done away with my old sofa-bed and have instead got a nice-looking sofa (just a two-seater, I might add).

"Hello, sweetheart. How are you?!" my mum greets, coming out of her bedroom, looking and smelling amazing.

Whatever effect this John is having on Mum, I really like it, I think as I watch my mum approach me, seemingly floating with arms opened wide. For the first time in a long time, Mum gives me a really big, warm hug.

"Are you staying for supper, Darla, or is this a flying visit?" John asks, beginning to get things out of the freezer.

My God, they even have the fridge freezer stocked with food. I am in total disbelief at how well organised Mum and John seem to flow together as a unit.

"Oh, yes. Please stay for supper," my mum begs playfully, doing her best puppy-dog impression sticking out her bottom lip.

Looking at her face, I cannot say no. "Yes, please. Supper would be lovely."

"Righto," John affirms, setting another plate into the oven.

Mum and I sit on the sofa, and I fill her in about my new dance opportunity, explaining that I am on a trial basis. We didn't part last time on the best of terms, and I wanted to smooth things over with her this time now that there had been space enough for the air to clear between us.

"That is fantastic news, darling. I'm so proud of you. Your gran and grandad would be so proud of you also."

I tell my mum about the glimmer of recognition my grandmother had when I last visited her in the home. Mum gets very emotional, which is to be expected, and she is very grateful that I'm stronger than she is to be able to go and visit her. My mum can't bear to see Gran's vacant expression and complete lack of recognition of who she is, so it is nice to inform Mum of some good news about my last visit.

"Fancy that—your gran remembering watching you dance ballet to that specific music track," Mum muses.

It is then my phone rings. Looking at it, I see it's an unknown caller, but I answer, guessing this may be Pink Club calling. I excuse myself to take the call outside. "Hello. Darla Pebble speaking," I answer in my best professional singsong voice.

"Hello, Darla, this is Eva Godstone. I have spoken to Joshua, and he has asked me to invite you down to Pink Club at 10:30 tomorrow morning. For security reasons, we will be sending one of our drivers to come and collect you."

"Oh, right…great…th-thank you."

"You're very welcome. And may I just express my apologies for my diabolical behaviour back at your audition," Eva continues in a gushing manner that makes my head spin. I'm not too sure how sincere she really is.

"That is very kind of you, thank you."

"Tomorrow when you arrive, I will go through your contract and show you around. Have you told anyone that you are going to be working for us?"

"No, I only told my mum I have had a dance opportunity, but she doesn't know where yet."

"I am asking that you not tell her. The fewer people who know about…our staff, the better."

"Ok, what should I tell her then?"

"I'll leave the details up to you, just don't mention Pink Club."

I thought this was a dance club, not MI5, I think at the bizarreness of the situation. After all, everyone knew Bella worked at the club. "I'm sure I can think of something. Why the sudden need for secrecy?" I ask, wondering or not if I'm pushing my luck with the questions.

"My big boss wishes to keep you an enigma. She feels it will add an extra layer of mystery to our nightclub and so make it more appealing for potential customers."

Interesting—the big boss is a woman, I think, absorbing this tid bit of info Eva has accidentally let slip.

"What is her name…the big boss, I mean?" I am then kicking myself inwardly as I feel I am pushing my luck.

"I will…let *her* fill you in when she undoubtedly meets you one day soon," Eva responds, being as vague as ever.

"Ok, is there anything else?"

"No, I think I've covered everything. See you tomorrow." Eva hangs up the phone before I can answer.

Sighing, I walk back into my mum and John's apartment, thankful to be back in the warmth, as it is getting jolly cold outside.

"Everything ok?" my mum asks as she puts the lasagne in the oven.

"That was just the dance company on the phone. It seems they have had a change of heart about the position," I answer, feeling uneasy about lying to my mum.

"I'm sorry to hear that, sweetie. Glass of wine?"

"I'll get that. You sit down," John puts in while indicating for me to sit at the small dining table.

By the time we have eaten supper and had a good catch up, it is soon time for me to be making a move. "This was nice. Hopefully we can do it again soon," I say, getting up to go.

"Do you have to leave already? I thought we could watch a movie," my mum pouts.

"Well, you do still owe me for the cinema date we missed. Rain check?" I offer and am glad to see my mother's face brighten.

"I will clear the plates away. It was good to see you again, Darla," John announces as he picks up the plates and walks them to the sink.

Out of habit, I offer to help to do the washing up, but John swiftly informs me they now have a dishwasher and so there is no need. On that note, I say my goodbye's, happy to see this new change in my mother.

John, you'd better not break my mother's heart or I will break you, I think as I make my way back out into the cold.

Waiting in the bus shelter for the last ride of the night, thoughts of just how much my life is about to change forever float around inside my head.

A group of three lads approach and I suddenly become very switched on the fact I am alone and now outnumbered if these three have ill intentions. Ever since my ex-boyfriend put me in the hospital over an argument about how I had made egg and chips instead of the steak he'd wanted after I forgot to defrost the steaks, I am now on edge whenever I'm alone and in the company of a strange man or men.

They are huddled together and laughing at something on one of their mobile phones. One of the men tries to get my attention and I choose to ignore him by putting my headphones on and listening to my music playlist. The young man, however, doesn't take being ignored well and puts a hand on my shoulder. Instinctively, using a move I learned on a self-defence weekend I went on with Sarah after my ex-boyfriend incident, I go into autopilot and throw him to the ground. He lands flat on his back, and the force of impact winds him. The other two men don't know what to do, and one begins yelling at me, so I hurriedly pretend to dial 999 and ask for police. The men pick their friend up and jog away, shouting back towards me that I am crazy. Just as they disappear from view, the bus arrives and hurriedly I climb aboard.

~ *Chapter 22* ~

Entering the apartment, I spot a bright post-it note on the fridge from Dante. **On a date. Won't be late. Champers in the fridge.**

Noticing the bottle of pink champagne in the fridge (the irony on choice of colour not lost on me), I decide to celebrate in a different way. I move the furniture to the far wall and begin dancing to a remixed version of *Halycon*. Thoughts of dancing at Pink Club enter my mind and the energy brings my soul to life.

I still can't believe I have the job. How is it even possible that my lifelong dream to dance professionally came about so fast? It is as if all the elements came together at just the right time to get me noticed and finally taken seriously.

"Whoop! Whoop!" I yell loudly as I dance.

Binks comes to join me, jumping onto the sofa against the far wall as if indicating that some food would be nice. I stop the music and stand, panting a while, feeling more alive I've felt in a long time.

"Hey, buddy, guess it's dinner time for you."

I put the furniture back in place and pour some fresh cat biscuits into Bink's little kitty bowl. I decide to wait for Dante and Sarah before breaking into the champagne. I'm not left waiting too long, however, as they both walk through the door soon after I've fed Binks.

"There she is, the superstar of the hour," Sarah announces. She is carrying a huge bouquet of flowers and heading over to give me a hug.

"Aw, thank you!" I exclaim, taking the flowers from her. I put them into the sink until I can designate a vase for them.

POP! Dante has opened the champagne and Sarah and I both jump while laughing. He then hands us a fancy looking champagne flute and swiftly pours the pink liquid into each one.

"Here is to a bright new future for Darla and many successful years with Pink Club."

"Here, here," Sarah affirms.

We gingerly chink glasses together and then swiftly down our champagne before Dante pours us another round. The rush of pink bubbles course through my body, giving me a nice, relaxed feeling that blossoms from my heart outwards.

Dante puts some dance music on and the three of us proceed to dance around like lunatics until flopping down on the sofa to catch our breath. Once we settle down, we decide to watch one of the dancing movie greats, *Dirty Dancing*.

Dante falls asleep with Sarah lying across his lap, and as the credits to the film begin to roll, I slowly get up so as not to rouse them. Gingerly, I take the blanket off the back of the sofa and place it over them. It is here in this moment that I realise I have two of the best friends anyone could ever wish for.

I decide to take a nice hot shower before climbing into my nice warm bed. Binks curls up at the foot of my bed and I drift off into a peaceful slumber with a big grin on my face.

Life is next level amazing right now and I just wish I could bottle this feeling, I think, as sleep envelopes me.

* * * * *

"Mmm, something smells good," I say, entering the kitchen and appreciating the familiar smells of a cooked breakfast.

"Rising stars require a breakfast of champions!" Dante brags, waving a spatula above his head.

"Aw, thank you. Where's Sarah?"

"She had to leave for work but wished you the best of luck."

Dante sets the plate of hot comfort food in front of me. There are cooked sausages, bacon, hash browns, fried eggs, tomatoes, and mushrooms.

"I'm off to remove the last bits of equipment out of the community centre's dance studio. Enjoy your breakfast and I will see you later," Dante tells me cheerfully while removing his apron. He then dons his leather jacket and swiftly vacates the apartment.

"See you later, and thanks again for breakfast," I call out.

Once I've finish eating, and feed Binks, I head to my bedroom to choose my outfit for the day. Not knowing if today will require any sort of dancing, I decide to wear my Blueberry dance trousers, T-shirt and hoodie. Blueberry is a big dance clothing company, and I was gifted my clothes on one of the nights at Lucifer's Haven when Blueberry came to do a drive for their products.

My trousers are black with a neon blue stripe up the side and the word ***Blueberry*** written alongside the stripe. My white T-shirt dons the same Blueberry name across the chest area, and the hoodie is electric blue with a black stripe running down the side of each arm and the word Blueberry again.

At exactly 10:30 a.m., there is a knock on the door. To my surprise, Eva Godstone is standing outside. The sight of her takes my breath away, as I had been expecting a driver or someone else to pick me up, not Pink Club's very own senior PR manager.

"Good morning, Darla. Are you ready to go, or do you need some more time?"

"No, no, I'm good; ready to rock 'n' roll."

"Excellent. I instructed my driver, Bruno, to keep the engine running so the car will be nice and warm. I am so sorry for my unprofessional and downright heartless behaviour at your audition yesterday, Darla. It has been very stressful at work, but that's no excuse. I was hoping we might start again and get this working relationship off on professional footing," Eva tells me as we walk towards the private limousine parked out front.

"I understand and I accept your apology," I respond, not quite sure what else to say.

"Thank you. I thought while on the drive back to Pink Club we could get to know each other better," Eva chatters while climbing into the back of the limousine.

The chauffeur introduces himself as Bruno, and holds the door open for us. It is only once we are both inside the warm car and have set off that I start to feel myself relaxing a bit more.

"Ah, that's better. *Brrrr,* its cold today! Now, Darla, tell me everything about you. Let's start with how you got into dancing."

I find chatting with Eva relatively easy to do once the ice is broken between us, and I see that under all her rough exterior she really is a sweetheart. I tell Eva of my journey through Busy Bee's, then the devastation of losing my grandparents, how I met Dante and how he got me into street dance and my job at Lucifer's Haven, to which Eva recoils ever so slightly on recognition that I have been a pole dancer.

"If its ok with you, I think we will...*not* mention to Joshua of your dancing lifestyle at...Lucifer's Haven...if that's ok with you?"

"That's fine with me," I agree, somewhat seeing Eva's point. Having met Joshua briefly two times now, I don't think that news would sit well with someone like him. I also suspect that he and this big boss lady were somehow responsible for me seeing a side to Eva that really does seem out of character now that I have the opportunity to sit and chat with her.

"How about you, Eva? Tell me something about yourself."

"Let's see...I graduated business studies in college with a distinction. I love PR and marketing. Pink Club is my biggest job so far, and—although times can be...difficult, such as what's just happened with Bella—it is, for the most part, good fun, so I can't complain. I was born in Bavaria but grew up in London when my parents emigrated over here for a better life. When I was twelve years old, I lost both my parents in a car crash and entered the U.K. fostering system until I was eighteen." Eva's voice falls away and a blank expression crosses her face as the memory seems to replay itself.

"I am so sorry you lost your parents under such tragic circumstances," I say, suddenly feeling guilty for all the times I have ever moaned about my own mother.

"Thank you. Oh, it looks like we have just arrived," Eva announces, instructing Bruno to go through to the underground car park.

~ *Chapter 23* ~

Once the car is parked and we exit out of the vehicle, I notice we are indeed in a massive underground parking space, empty but for a few cars dotted about. Eva takes out a key card and holds it over a panel next to lift doors. A green light comes on with a 'ping' and the doors open. The man I saw with Joshua at Chef No. 9 and at my audition appears from behind the lift doors, holding his arm out, indicating for us to step inside.

"Maxwell," Eva greets.

"Miss Godstone, Miss Pebble," the man I now know to be Maxwell says.

The lift is huge and includes mirrors and a pink plush sofa studded with diamantés. *Pretty Woman, indeed.* The lift reminds me of a famous scene from the movie.

"Oh, before I forget…here." Eva pulls a piece of paper from her jacket pocket. It is a disclaimer for me to sign that says I will never mention to anyone what I have seen in Pink Club, along with a load of legal clauses. Once I have the gist of the document, I happily sign it with a pink pen that Eva hands me.

"I will need to borrow Miss Pebble at some point today to sort out her security passes," Maxwell says.

"Of course," Eva replies, placing the signed form inside her jacket pocket.

As I watch Eva, I take in her outfit. She's wearing a charcoal grey suit with pastel pink pin stripes all over it. On her feet are two very inappropriate wintertime shoes which are pink pastel kitten heels. Her hair is pulled up in an ornate hairdo. On her wrist is a very expensive-looking Rolex watch, and her hands are attractively decorated with expertly made acrylic pink nails.

"Wait….what about my friends who accompanied me to my audition. Won't they –"

"It has all been taken care of. They both signed disclaimer forms while you took a five-minute break after my…little outburst," Eva admits, blushing.

Before I can respond, the lift comes to a stop and Maxwell places a hand on a scanner above the lift buttons. We are then granted entry inside. Once the doors open, the scene before me takes my breath away for the second time today.

"Impressive, eh?" Eva gives me a knowing smile.

We walk out into a dimly-pink-lit corridor covered in a pink fluffy carpet that makes your feet feel light and bouncy as you walk on it, and the walls are adorned in French boutique-styled black and pink wallpaper. Pink lights of faux pink candles line the walls with low level pink lighting to give the space a very heady feel.

Geez, they were not kidding when they named this place 'Pink' Club, I humorously muse to myself.

"I have a few security checks to do, but if I can just borrow Darla's index finger before you guys dash off…" Maxwell gently and expertly lifts my hand, then clamps a painless device around my index finger momentarily before removing it. "That is your fingerprint recognition stored. Now for your visual cortex…look this way, please." Maxwell holds up a flat screen device and I look straight ahead as a bright flash goes off, creating dots that swim about in my vision. "All done. See you ladies again later. Oh, and please call me Max, Darla. Do you have any preference to what I should call you?"

"Darla is fine, thank you," I tell him as I blink the remaining dots away.

"I think first I will give you the grand tour and then introduce you to everyone. You already know Octavia, but you'll be meeting your backing dancers today. They will be responsible for your safety on the dance stage," Eva explains once Max leaves.

"Sounds ominous…the stage, I mean."

We exit the corridor and walk through two double doors into a different area. "Woah! This is so cool!" I exclaim. The sight before me almost quite literally has my jaw hitting the floor.

"This is the reception area where we receive all of our guests for whatever function they have come to attend. We have eleven entertainment rooms in total, so you will never be short of work here."

The space is massive. White and pink marble pillars and an enormous, fancy-looking reception desk fill the front area. A Juliette staircase takes centre stage with a bright pink carpet running all the way down the white rounded marble steps on either side. Pale pink crystal chandeliers hang high on the crisp, white ceiling.

Directly opposite the reception area is a set of double doors which gives the illusion of an outdoor entryway to a pub.

"That is The Pelican Brief Bar," Eva announces proudly. "Joshua is a big fan of that film, so Mimi decided to dedicate this space to her brother."

The windows are quite dark, so it's difficult to see inside, but Eva promises to bring me here later today once all the formalities are over.

"Is Joshua here?" I ask, feeling suddenly alarmed as to why I should even ask such a question that really is none of my business.

"Errmm, no. Joshua has been a bit of a ghost around here since Mimi died. Right, I think it's time I introduce you to your backing dance team. Octavia should be rehearsing with them so let's go and say hello."

"It sounded absolutely tragic in the press about what happened to Joshua's sister. I remember seeing it all unfold on the news." Again, the words just roll out before I can stop them.

"Yes, it came as quite a shock to everyone," Eva says, her clipped sombre tone suggesting she wants to get off the topic.

We ascend the left-hand side of the Juliette staircase and walk along another ornately decorated corridor, only this one has much brighter lighting and there are framed photographs and posters of previous Pink Club events.

"Woah! Is that —"

"Queenie, yes, but *shhh*—mum's the word. It's one of Pink Club's greatest achievements and well-kept secrets," Eva says with a grin.

As we reach the end of the corridor, I notice the last door on the left has a plaque on it that reads J. Glass, Managing Director. My cheeks blush as a flash of his rogue and a handsome face comes to the forefront of my mind. Horrified at my gaga response to seeing his name, I swiftly push all thoughts of Joshua Glass aside. *Get a grip, Darla; keep the hormones in check, woman,* I think, now trying to keep my head out of the gutter. My sexual goddess wants nothing more than to plunge straight into my deepest darkest fantasies with Joshua Glass, if only to imagine acting out all the lustful images that now threaten to overwhelm my psyche.

We round a corner off to the right, and my reverie of lustful wanton thoughts of Joshua Glass is broken, as I can now hear the familiar *thud-thud-thud* of dance music. We walk a little further and a dance studio comes into view to our left. Through two crystal clear glass doors I can see there are indeed dancers within, going through their paces.

Octavia spots us and hurriedly stops the music before jogging over to greet us. "Well, hey, pretty lady. Come in, come in," she says, ushering me inside a room of sweaty male dancers.

Gulp!

"I take it Darla will be alright with you for a while. I have some errands to run for *his majesty.*" Eva hands me over to Octavia.

I am not sure if it is the lighting in the studio, but just before Eva leaves, she gives me a tired smile and I can't help but notice the dark circles under her eyes; she looks exhausted.

"Don't worry, we will take good care of our latest protégé," Octavia assures her, giving me an excitable grin as she gently draws me into the dance studio.

Eva pitter patters away at speed with those cute pink kitten heels she is wearing. I now can't take my eyes off the sight befalling me.

Eenie, meenie, miney, mo…bubba, have I died and gone to Heaven? I now have such a big feast of very hot-looking men in front of me, and my nether regions all but feel like they may explode. *It's official: I'm a slut!*

"Darla, I'd like you to meet your safety dance team. We have Midnight, a retired cirque performer whose skills have come in very useful since he moved to the U.K. and began lending us his knowledge on how to best perform safely on raised staging platforms."

I shake one of Midnight's dark-skinned hands and it feels as if his amazing dark eyes see right through my very soul and naughty thoughts. *Once you go black, you never—no! No more naughty thoughts. Bad, naughty thought—keep it clean,* I tell myself, trying my best to unscramble my now very *drunk-on-lust* mind.

"Pleased to meet you, Darla. And if it's any consolation, you're much prettier in the flesh than on TV," Midnight jokes.

At first, I wonder what he means before the penny drops…'*Blow job girl.*' Mortified, I wait for Octavia to introduce the other dancers, praying none of the other men refer to my Chef No. 9 *faux pas,* and I'm glad to see that they don't.

By the end of the introductions, I have learned the names and information of the rest of the team, my lustful thoughts now firmly on ice after Midnight's little quip!

Siren is a retired police officer who picked up dancing while he was on the force and took it up as a profession after an injury in the line of duty saw his police career finished early. He has ash blonde hair and piercing blue eyes.

Medley is a musician at heart but also loves to dance. He takes pride in being able to perform professionally on the pianos that are dotted about Pink Club. Medley is the smallest in build to all the other men and quite a camp character, so I'm guessing he may have a boyfriend on the scene. Such a waste for all the female populous if he *is* gay, though, because boy if he isn't tall, dark and handsome.

Digit is a computer whizz, college dropout and looks vaguely familiar. I'm tempted to ask if he knows Dante but decide to keep it to myself since the club wants me to keep all this private. Digit confessed to knowing street dance as his only style, and not much else, which is where Octavia has been working with him to broaden his skills. Digit has no hair, but like the rest, he has washboard abs where I also notice a small scar on his upper right abdominal area.

Finally, I was introduced to a guy called Mixer. I'm informed that Mixer is a professional bartender/mixologist and sometimes works both the bar and the dance floors here at Pink Club. Mixer has a wild mane of dreadlocks and seems to be the most chilled out member of the group.

"Well, it's certainly nice to meet all of you. I am so sorry about Bella's death, and how awful to think I'm her replacement. You guys must have been a close-knit team," I say, putting my mouth into full babble mode before I can stop myself.

"It is a damn shame what happened to Lady Blitz, but alas, I think we can all agree she had one heck of a drug problem. Let's all count our blessings she didn't die while during a show," Midnight says in his rich Caribbean accent, which washes over me like the hypnotically soothing wave of the ocean—though I detect a clip in his tone.

The rest of the men just nod in response before they begin

collecting their things and heading towards the studio doors.

"Was it something I said?" I turn to Octavia who looks less than pleased at the frosty reception I have just been given by my so-called safety dance team.

"They'll come around, especially once they see you dance," Octavia tells me with a wink, which does nothing to allay my fears of not being accepted by these men.

"Come on. Seeing as Eva is now busy, I want to give you the grand tour. Be prepared to be blown away." Octavia links her arm through mine and we head out of the dance studio.

~ *Chapter 24* ~

Joshua sits in his luxury apartment on the top floor of his parents'
hotel which is named "The Mimi Glass Hotel," set up after his sister's
murder. They had actually been in the process of buying a hotel around
the time she was killed. The memories of their daughter, however,
would prove too painful, and as they had a holiday home in Tuscany,
Joshua's parents sold up and moved there permanently once his father
retired, leaving the overseeing of the hotel to Joshua. The relationship
with his parents had become strained since their daughter's death; they
couldn't believe Joshua hadn't seen any red flags from this so-called
boyfriend of hers. Now Joshua only saw his parents for Mimi's
birthday when he would fly there to mark the occasion as a sense of
duty to his mum and dad. But as tensions ran high—especially between
him and his father—his visits, which once were long and much looked
forward too while Mimi had been alive, had now become brief flying
visits while visiting his parents. The lonely plane rides over-exacerbated
the fact that Mimi was no longer alive, which were bad enough, but
the broken-down frosty reception he would get from his parents now,
along with the awkward atmosphere, seemed worse.

Their parents had been against Joshua and Mimi's dancing venture idea, hoping they would have graduated from some prestigious university with a degree in something akin to that of becoming a doctor or solicitor. When they'd learned of the financial troubles Joshua and Mimi were having to get their business off the ground after graduating from a performing arts college, their mum and dad had hoped it would mean an end to the 'silly dream' as they called it, but when a mysterious beneficiary came on scene, helping them put it together, which jettisoned Pink Club to the success it has become, Joshua and Mimi's parents just couldn't accept that it would ever work.

After Mimi was killed by her boyfriend, resentment about the club spilled over and the resentment was aimed at Joshua. In a heated argument at Mimi's funeral, everyone witnessed Joshua's dad, James, spitting venom at his son, blaming him for her death by saying Joshua should have taken better care of Mimi and protected her. His mother, Pandora, tried to settle the rift, but the damage was done, and the wounds administered by Frank's sharp tongue cut very deep. Their father-son relationship had never recovered to anywhere near what it was. This hurt Joshua very deeply, as they used to be such a close-knit family unit.

"Hi, Max. Have you run all the security checks on Miss Pebble?" Joshua asks over the phone to his valued bodyguard, friend, and head of security.

"I can indeed assure you that I have checked and double checked on your new leading dance lady, and she is clean, happy to report—no criminal record. However, there was something minor on her mother, Rumer Pebble."

"Interesting...I'm sure you'll send me over all the relevant details?"

"Certainly, sir."

"Thanks, Max, that will be all." Joshua hangs up, now pondering his new employee's mother.

The sight of Darla Pebble on her knees in front of him would not leave him, and then to watch her dance so passionately on stage stirred emotions in him much the same as he would feel when his heart would swell watching his sister Mimi dance. But Mimi never turned Joshua on because that would have both been gross and incestuous. Darla, though...there was just something about her he couldn't shake. She had gotten under his skin, and both times he had laid eyes on her, it awoke something in him that had long since faded away from overwhelming grief: his sex drive. The thoughts troubled and confused him deeply. Joshua now found himself wanting to know if she were single or involved with someone. He could ask Max, but that would make it far too obvious...or would it?

Joshua picks the phone back up and dials.

"Max, I need to bother you again."

"Not a problem at all, sir. Go ahead."

Joshua pauses and takes a breath before asking Max to find out if Darla had any man on the scene as in *romantically,* saying he didn't want any outside complications to her application process. After Max tells Joshua she is well and truly single, Joshua's thoughts about her and his new peaked interest in wanting to know more begin to re-surface, troubling him further.

"Thank you, Max. I look forward to receiving the file."

"Roger that. Is there anything else I can help you with?"

"Not right now. I'll be in touch." Joshua hangs up.

CCTV cameras from within Pink Club get live streamed to Joshua's computer at home. It was Stella's idea to make sure that there was an outside link to Pink Club at all times with Joshua, as he had decided to step back from being a regular presence there since Mimi's murder. Watching everything running smoothly within its secret walls, Joshua starts to close down his laptop until he notices Darla being shown around by Octavia. He is glad to see someone is showing her around, which begs the question…where is Eva?

Checking all the cameras, Joshua eventually locates her. She is asleep on the floor of her office. He makes a mental note to remember to insist that Eva get a holiday as soon as possible, as it will be a disaster if she ends up exhausted to the point where mistakes start being made.

* * * * *

"Ok, be prepared to be amazed," Octavia declares with a glint in her eye.

We have descended a small alleyway that is painted in dark blue, and there are paintings of whales and undersea creatures as we go. In front of us are two ornately decorated gold doors with handles made to look like two big tridents. I wait with bated breath to see what's behind the doors to the first of eleven rooms that I now know exist here at Pink Club.

Oh…my! The sight before me took my breath away. "This is…this is…wow! It's a real-life *AQUARIUM!*" I cry, noting that we have entered a tunnel with a glass roof and walls full of exotic tropical fish

129

swimming above and around us.

"Impressive, right? This is the octopus lounge; we even have our own personal mermaids."

"Shut the front door! Mermaids!"

"Yes, indeed. These women are expertly skilled in how to swim with those big realistic-looking mermaid tails. I would give it a go, but I'm…terrified of deep water," Octavia admits. I feel humbled she has opened up to me with her fear.

As if on cue, two women come swimming up to the side of this huge tank (the side without the sharks in, I notice) and give a little dance for us before swimming off.

"This is so surreal!"

Next, we wander on to the lounge area which, indeed, lives up to its name. There are golden pillars with massive golden octopuses wrapped around them. The carpet is a deep dark purple colour, and there is a beautiful golden piano where a man sits. He is wearing a top hat and tails and is playing a dreamy tune. A bar designed to look like it's made from living coral reef sits off to the right, with cute little golden octopus bar stools that don plush purple cushioning. Booths are dotted about for guests to sit in—again, wrapped in the same deep dark purple upholstery with golden tables.

"Right, come on. We've no time to dilly-dally. There are many more rooms to check out before we land back at The Pelican Brief Bar, and I don't know about you, but I am famished," Octavia says, rubbing her stomach.

"Now that you mention it, I am a little peckish myself…and thirsty."

"Gizmo, please get our guest and new star of the house a Sea Shanty."

"Certainly, ma'am. Anything for yourself?" Gizmo asks Octavia.

I take in Gizmo's look. He is a sharply dressed character who wears a purple waistcoat, tight-fitting black trousers and a long-sleeve white shirt. His hair is gelled back, and he looks every bit the professional barman for such a highly esteemed and well-respected nightclub.

"No, thank you. I'm still on the clock."

"What's in it…exactly?" I ask tentatively, realising there's alcohol involved with it.

"You know, I don't actually know, ha-ha. I just know that it's bright blue with crushed ice and tastes very *yummy*."

This does not fill me with confidence, but I accept my Sea Shanty graciously and begin to carefully sip through the purple straw. Octavia was not joking when she said it was bright blue. Why, it's practically glowing in the dark, it's so luminous. The flavour is exquisite and I can't really taste any alcohol, so I pace myself so I don't get caught out and begin acting silly in front of Octavia or other staff here.

"Next up, the Flamingo Lounge," Octavia announces while looping her arm through mine and steering me out of the Octopus room.

"This place is like a maze. How on earth do you not get lost?"

"Ah, yes, you will require a map. Remind me to ask Eva to give you one when we meet her back at The Pelican Brief Bar."

'So, this is really quite a big place then? Funny, from the outside it just looks like a moderately-sized square building.'

"And therein lies the illusion. We go deep underground and there isn't an inch of the building space above that isn't also filled up with Pink Club pizazz."

"No wonder you have such a tight security team."

"Thankfully, our big boss has fingers in many, *many* pies. After all, she *is* married to an Arabian millionaire yacht salesman."

"I knew the big boss lady was a woman, but I had no idea –"

"Bugger, I've said to much. Please don't let onto Eva that you know that."

"Your secret is safe with me," I reassure Octavia.

"She would literally fry my ass if she knew I'd let the intimate details of the big boss out. Let's just say she likes to remain in the background, as in *only here to mingle not to manage*."

"Honestly, it's forgotten about already. I can't wait to see The Flamingo Lounge," I say, getting us back on track.

~ *Chapter 25* ~

The Pink Flamingo Lounge is amazing. A round, bright pink centre stage stands lined with square-shaped reflective mirror fragments around its base. I'm happy to see a pole off to the back of the stage area; I instantly feel on familiar ground. The entire room is decorated wall to ceiling in bright pink tones and accents.

"Wait, where are the seats?" I wonder aloud while looking around.

"This is a Jacuzzi room." Octavia says this like it's the most normal thing I should have expected to come out of her mouth.

"A *Jacuzzi* room?"

"Those, right there, are Jacuzzis." Octavia points around us, and then I notice there are indeed Jacuzzis dotted about with pink lights inside of them, the water bubbling calmly within each pool.

"Wow—remind me to bring my swimming costume next time."

"It was Mimi's pride and joy. She thought about bringing all the loveliness of spa Jacuzzis to a room where people could also be thoroughly entertained."

My Sea Shanty is zinging all throughout my body now with the all too familiar buzz I feel after an alcoholic beverage. "I don't see a bar,"

I say, wondering how people get served in here.

Octavia indicates for me to follow her around a pink glass partition made with square cubes of glass. On the other side, there is a pink swimming pool with a bar in the middle.

"The bar is *in* the swimming pool?!"

"Uh-huh. Mimi was inspired when she stayed in a high-end Maltese hotel that had a bar where guests had to swim up to in order to get their drinks."

"She did a good job. So, this big boss lady of yours…what did she do, just give free designing rights over to Joshua and Mimi?"

"Well, Stella shafted Joshua after they had…you know, got together, and by the time he found out she had, erm…yes, yes, all designing rights were given to Joshua and Mimi," Octavia says, rushing the last part of the garbled sentence. It seemed again that suddenly she realised her mistake of saying too much.

Mental note: Never tell Octavia anything private, I think, realising she seems to let a lot of cats out of a lot of bags.

"It's amazing you keep so quiet about this place," I say sarcastically, grinning at Octavia.

"Ha-ha, yeah I see your point there. You'll learn the story one day undoubtedly, but you know…for now it's hush-hush."

"Yes, I know—*don't tell Eva.*"

"Thank you. I really love talking to you. Bella was never one for mingling with any of us; all she cared about was getting her money and rubbing shoulders with celebrities. You are a breath of fresh air, Darla. Promise me you will not change."

"I promise. Which room is next?" I ask excitedly, imagining what other delights I've yet to discover.

The next room Octavia takes me to is called The Genie Lamp. The doors to this room are designed to look like they have been imbedded into the side of a cavern.

"Make a wish. I know it's probably silly, but I always like to close my eyes and make one before entering this room," Octavia tells me.

I follow her lead, standing still a moment, eyes closed, taking in a deep breath before making my own wish.

The room we enter is very cavern-like, and faux gems are imbedded into the walls. There are booths dotted around in the curved parts of the room. It is then I notice the ground is moving beneath me.

"Oops! Forgot you'll need to take your shoes off for this room…that's real sand."

We park our shoes by the entryway doors and re-enter the room with bare feet. The sand feels cool between my toes. I lose sight of Octavia momentarily as bright lights come on and blink rapidly from the sudden change of going from darkness to light.

"These are high-tech sunshine lights. Doesn't the space look and feel very desert-like?" Octavia asks, moving forward to twirl in what I'm guessing is centre stage.

I notice large, ornate curtains hanging down with shades of bright pinks and turquoise. The backdrop is a magical oasis in the middle of a desert. On the centre of every table is a lamp much like a genie lamp. I am informed by Octavia that guests write their wishes on paper and drop them into the lamps, and then they are burned, as if the wishes are being released to the universe.

"This is one of my favourite themed rooms, and it's also very popular when we have guests visiting from the Middle East, namely royalty. We give them a feel of home away from home. Pink Club boasts one of the best belly dancing troupes in the world, and I have to say—having watched them perform—they truly are a sight to behold." Octavia's voice is dreamy as she stares off into nowhere.

"Cool. It is quite mind-boggling how you've managed to tuck this all away and out of sight of regular everyday Londoners. No wonder you keep it all highly secure. But how do you stop people from blabbing?"

"We have a hefty contract for people to sign before they are allowed inside, and all mobile phone and tech devices are taken off everyone upon entering so there's no risk of leaked photos or video footage. We've had the odd journalist trying their luck, but Max and his team are so good that they don't even get past the secure car park gates before being turned away."

"It sounds similar to Area 51" I say, grinning at just how insane the place is and what I'm now finding myself involved in.

"Speaking of which...come on." Octavia grabs my hand and gently pulls me out of the genie room.

We shake the sand off our feet and slip our shoes back on. Soon we are back in a part of the night club that has the pink lights and fluffy pink carpets. The faux pink candles that line the walls cause me to feel enveloped, as if by an invisible loving hug.

"Now *this* room is a sight to behold. It's called The Conspirators' Bar. I have a love-hate relationship with it. It's almost as if it shouldn't be in here, but the guests love it...namely the two actors from that infamous UFO TV series from the 90's —"

"Get out! M & S have been here?!!"

"The very same. Of course, when they visit here, they are just themselves: Gillian and David. Chris has also graced us with his presence on occasion."

"I am a *huge* fan of that show. Wish I could meet them someday," I confess. I am now officially on cloud nine as my inner nerd sings from hearing this exciting bit of in-house information.

"You may just get your wish."

"What do you mean?"

"They *may* just be on the guest list for your big debut this spring at the gala."

"Oh, boy. I think I'm going to pass out." I feign a swooning motion and Octavia laughs.

We enter a room that is every bit as Area 51-ish as you'd think it would be. There's no performing stage in this room, and I'm told it is another one of their themed bars. Everything is monochrome silver and alien green. Road signs mimicking those found at Area 51 are displayed on the walls. A lava lamp sits on each of the tables and playing from speakers on the wall are soundtracks to most alien and Sci-Fi movies.

"Hang on a sec; Eva is calling," Octavia tells me, stepping away for some privacy. She soon reappears and tells me that we will have to continue the tour tomorrow because my contract is now ready and there are some final security bits and pieces that need tying up.

~ *Chapter 26* ~

Octavia has dropped me off outside Eva's office, and as I lift my hand to knock on her door—which I notice is very plain dark wood—she opens it with force from the other side, making us both jump.

"So sorry, Darla. Please, do come in." Eva stands to one side, inviting me into the warm space by indicating with an open-handed gesture.

The feel of her office is really welcoming. The colours are quite masculine, though, which I'm surprised to see. It's all magnolia and dark browns. I then discover the security guard, Max, to be also inside her office and he gives me a cheery smile.

"Please, take a seat." Eva indicates to one of the comfortable-looking dark brown reclining faux suede chairs.

Ooh, that's comfy, I think as I sink into its upholstery.

"Here is a copy of your contract. Don't read it now, as there's far too much in there. I suggest thinking of it as your homework. Once you've read it and bring it back here tomorrow—*signed*—then we can actually begin your training."

"Training?" I am suddenly perplexed. What is she talking about?

"For the stage, of course. It's why you have a dance safety team—to stop you from falling forty feet to your death. Did Octavia not explain any of this to you?" A frown is forming behind a pink pair of framed glasses Eva now dons, which matches her outfit perfectly.

What the...? My DEATH?! My heart now rapidly gallops away, making me appear slightly breathless.

"Listen, don't worry about it. Everything you need to know is in your contract. Put it out of your mind."

Put it out of my mind?! Are you insane, woman? You've just told me I'll be performing on a stage that could KILL ME! "Sure, ok...no problem," comes my actual response, as my head now swims with fear.

"Right, now that you have your contract, I need to give you your security passes," Max says, giving me a much-needed distraction from my now-racing thoughts and imagined images of falling to my doom.

I'm expecting an actual key card like the one I saw Eva use on the lift before we entered Pink Club, but to my amazement I'm given a bracelet.

"This bracelet is disguised to look like a piece of jewellery. You also have this key card. If you lose your card, then you just have to hold your wrist with the bracelet over any of the security locks and it should gain you access if your code is accepted."

"This is so cool!" I exclaim, feeling very secret spy-ish indeed. "How do guests get about then?"

"Each of our guests has a special temporary badge, and every time they enter or leave a room, a ping gets sent off to security cameras and team back at the hub," Eva responds smoothly.

"When you remove your bracelet, you *must* keep the items within this secure box," Max tells me, and then hands me an unassuming locked black metal box.

"Gee, I'm surprised it isn't pink!"

"We wanted to make the boxes look as uninteresting as possible to avoid theft of them."

"I see how that makes sense."

"Right, well, if you are all done with the security for Darla, I need to go through some of the perks she now has as a senior working member of Pink Club," Eva says to Max, indicating that she wants us to be left alone.

Max leaves us and Eva takes me towards the The Pelican Brief Bar.

"Once your contract is signed and brought back here tomorrow, I will arrange for people to come and collect your belongings from where you currently live, and –"

"Pardon?" I interrupt, suddenly feeling as if the rug has been pulled out from under me.

"Your new accommodation…it's part of the package. Now, it *is* the same apartment where Bella was found…you know, dead…but it really is a beautiful piece of property and I'm confident that once you see it you won't be able to say no."

I'm shocked into stunned silence, not quite sure how I feel or how to process this new information. *My own luxury apartment! What the EFF just happened?!*

"Right, erm –"

"I know, it's a lot to process. Even *I* have my own Pink Club premises; it helps with security. All bills are also covered by our big boss."

140

"That's…well…" I can't seem to form sentences or words properly, as my mouth has gone as dry as sandpaper.

"You look as hungry as I feel. Come on, let's grab some lunch and get to know each other better. I am, after all, your PR manager now."

Wow, how has my head not exploded yet? I think as Eva opens the doors to The Pelican Brief Bar.

A warm welcoming wave of air greets us from an overhead unit. Inside, the place looks like an old-fashioned American bar, and staff wander about in old, classic-style-looking and very smart uniforms. A man with fiery cropped red hair and a moustache stands behind the bar polishing glasses. The smells of pub lunch make my stomach grumble loudly.

"Someone's hungry, I take it," Eva laughs. I am glad to see a happier side to her persona.

"Ha-ha, yeah. There has to be something wrong if you smell good old-fashioned pub grub and can't form an appetite," I giggle, rubbing my tummy. I'm almost salivating at the mere prospect of chunky chips and something nice and meaty to sink my teeth into, like a nice piece of rump or sirloin.

We sit at a table near a window that has a faux image painted on it of passing traffic on a busy city street. There are green palms dotted about and a juke box tucked away in one corner. Iconic moments of the movie "The Pelican Brief" are hung on the walls, and—on closer inspection—I can see that they are autographed.

"Ah, that's better," Eva says, letting her hair down from its previously ornate up-do. "What's on the menu today, Eric?" she calls out to the red-haired gentleman at the bar.

"Chef's specials are Stilton and broccoli soup for starter, beef Wellington for main, and…American cheesecake for pudding."

"Do people frequent this place when there are not big shows on? I got the impression –"

"That's the beauty of the place. It's completely inclusive for the members who sign up for an annual VIP membership to enjoy entertainment any day of the week. We only get *noticed* when the big events are on, as we get an unusually higher than normal volume of celebs who just *love* to boost their profile by letting the world know they are living it large in London. People can *literally* come here to enjoy good food and entertainment with the general public and media being none the wiser," Eva explains, having cut me off.

"So, I might actually meet…celebrities…at *any time?*"

"Indeed, which is why I insist you bring an autograph book with you. I already have several full ones tucked away at home. Now, what to have for lunch? I think I'll have the special today. You seem like a steak and chips gal to me, am I right?"

"Talk about hitting the nail on the head." I shake my head, amazed at Eva's spot-on assumption. I feel I am going to have to watch myself around this one.

Eva gives our orders to Eric, and we are soon enjoying our food, which gives me a break and the chance for things to start sinking in. Once we finish eating, Eva charges the bill to Pink Club's account, where she informs me that staff must buy their own lunch but do get a discount.

"I think we have covered a lot today. Just read your contract *thoroughly* and bring it with you tomorrow. Is it ok if I arrange a car to come and pick you up a bit earlier?"

"Sure—and thank you so much for this opportunity. It means…more than words could ever say."

"Don't be silly; you've earned your spot here fair and square. The very fact that Joshua liked your dancing says a lot…*believe* me. He is not in the business of hiring just any Tom, Dick or Harry. No, he is quite particular on who he does and doesn't have working here."

"Octavia mentioned a map that I would need to help me navigate around here?" I question, suddenly remember Octavia's recommendation I ask Eva for a map.

"I will print one off for you tomorrow. Sorry I wasn't able to give you a complete tour, but tomorrow I have made some free time to take you around the rest of the entertainment rooms here." Eva is smiling warmly at me. She really isn't too bad once I get to know her.

A call is put into Max, and all too soon it's time for me to leave. I'm handed back my mobile phone and bag, then escorted back to the underground carpark by Max.

By the time I re-enter Dante's apartment, I am exhausted from all the excitement of the day. Checking my mobile straight away, I notice have about five missed calls from Mum. I'm now worried, as this is very unusual, and my gut says something terrible must have happened.

"Darla? Oh, thank goodness! I have been worried sick!" my mum cries, sounding genuinely sincere. The tone of my mother's voice now lets me know that my gut instinct was right.

"I'm fine. Sorry I didn't answer my phone. It's my new…err, job. No phones allowed while working policy."

"That explains why I couldn't raise you at Chef No. 9 or Lucifer's

Haven then."

"Wait? *What?* You called them?!" I exclaim, now feeling panicky.

"Thanks for the heads up about resigning so soon! Anyway, I'm calling because…because your grandmother passed away early this morning."

My mother's words slice through me like the sharpest of knives, and the breath in my body instantly leaves me. I find it a struggle to both breathe and remain standing.

"Sweetheart, are you there? Did you hear me?"

I take a moment to compose myself before being able to draw enough air in to reply. "Yeah…yes, I heard you. I…have to go. Sorry, Mum, call you later."

I hang up the call and silently slide to the floor, hugging my knees as wave after wave of grief washes over me.

~ *Chapter 27* ~

Dante arrives with Chinese takeaway for him and Sarah. "Oh…sorry, Darla, I didn't realise you'd be back already. Would you like to share our takeaway?" Dante says sounding embarrassed.

"I've actually eaten already but thanks. I'm going to hit the sack early."

"Hold up. I know that face and those red-rimmed eyes all too well. Come here and sit down. You are not leaving until you tell me what's happened," Dante instructs. I'm annoyed at him being right.

I tell him about my amazing day at Pink Club but not giving him any intimate details. I add the fact that I'll be moving out, and then I tell him about my grandmother's death. I then burst into a whole new fresh batch of tears just as Sarah enters, as if on cue.

"Oh, my God! What on earth has happened?!" Sarah exclaims, rushing over to Dante and me.

"Her gran passed away," Dante explains solemnly.

"Oh, honey…I am so very, very sorry. Can I do anything? Do you need anything?"

"Just…a…a…hug," I stammer, now wailing as I reach my arms

out to Sarah.

Once I have got over this recent wave of emotion, Sarah helps me to my bedroom while Dante goes to sort out their supper. We sit on my bed for a while, and I tell Sarah about my day at Pink Club. She tells me she will help me and read through the contract with Dante after they've eaten, insisting that I take some time to myself. Once Sarah leaves, and I am alone with my thoughts again, I sigh deeply and reach for my mobile to call my mother back.

"Hello, Darla. Darling, are you alright?"

"Yes, sorry, it was just a big shock. What happens now? When is the funeral? How did she die?" So many questions now plague my mind.

"Your gran passed peacefully in her sleep, and a woman named Matilda asked me to let you know she didn't have any pain…her heart just stopped."

"That's a…relief," I say through fresh bouts of tears.

"John has been helping me with the funeral arrangements. Your gran had a funeral plan which has helped a lot, but I wanted you to help me choose the flowers. It's late now, so I'll send you the link to the florist. Choose whichever ones you would like, and I'll add them to the arrangements, ok?"

"Ok. How are *you* doing?"

"To be honest, I'm sad—of course I am—but also a little bit relieved to know she's not suffering anymore in confusion. Does that make me a bad person?"

"No, Mum, it doesn't. I feel the same."

"She wouldn't want us to be sad. Tell you what, let me know when your next day off from this new job of yours is and we will arrange to finally go on our cinema date…ok?"

My mum saying this makes me feel good for a change. *It feels like she's beginning to be the parent again. Moving out seems really was the best thing,* I think, happy I made the right call.

"Sure, yeah, I'd love that."

"Ok, that's settled then. I'll send you the details of her funeral once it's all finalised."

"Thanks, Mum. I love you."

"Love you too, sweetheart."

We hang up the call and then I saunter out of my bedroom, now wearing my grey, fluffy winter penguin pyjamas and feeling puffy eyed and tired. All previous excitement of my first day at Pink Club has evaporated and is now replaced by a heavy blanket of grief at having just lost my grandmother.

"Oh, sweetie, I am again so very sorry for your loss," Sarah says as she opens her arms once more for a hug.

"Stop it or you'll set me off again and I need a clear head to go through this sodding block of a contract."

We all sit around the kitchen bar going one page at a time over all the clauses and agreements, some of which include:

1. No smoking in, around, or near Pink Club.
2. No staff romances. If romances develop, one—or both—parties must resign from their positions.
3. Employees must agree to regular drug testing.
4. Dressing appropriately is a must when out of costume so as to not offend any guests visiting the establishment.

5. Be kind and courteous to other members of staff.

6. Bullying and abuse of any kind is seen as an immediate dismissal offence.

For most part, it's all just common-sense mundane things that mostly all business contracts have. There is a section, however, for me about the risks involved with the part of my job that involves dancing forty feet in the air on a staging area. By signing the contract, I'm agreeing that if any accidents were to happen, Pink Club would not be implicated or be held responsible for any legal or medical costs as participants willingly dance knowing the risks.

My stomach rolls reading this part, but Dante assures me it will be fine, and that if it was really that dangerous then Bella Fitzroy wouldn't have been up there. Dante also tells me that the dancers are very skilled, having danced and performed with Joshua and company when they all attended the same performing arts college.

"Oh, I almost forgot!" Sarah cries as she reaches into her handbag. "The staff at Chef No. 9 did a whip round for your sudden departure, and, well…I know it's not much, but we couldn't let you go without saying goodbye." Sarah hands me a pretty, pink envelope.

Opening my card, I begin to feel tears again. Every staff member had signed the card, which is white with pretty, multi-coloured butterflies splattering the front and gold writing that says in big bold letters **GOOD LUCK!** Inside is a gift card for £150 to spend on a meal at Chef No. 9.

"This is…thank you so much! I think I'll treat my mum and her new boyfriend, John, to the meal voucher," I say, giving Sarah a hug.

"You're so welcome. Right, well, time is marching on and –"

"Are you not staying the night?" Dante asks sombrely.

"Don't worry; I have my ear plugs at the ready," I joke.

Sarah agrees to stay the night, and after I sign my life away on my new Pink Club contract, I head off to bed.

~ *Chapter 28* ~

The next morning, I stretch out in my double bed and take in the room I'm currently residing in for, perhaps, the last time.

'Bing, bong'. I hear the doorbell ring and drag myself out of bed, sleepily sauntering across the apartment to see who it is.

"Mmmmm, what now?"

I peek through the peephole and am not prepared to see Eva Godstone standing on the other side of the door. *Holy shit!* After taking a deep breath, I slide the lock across and open the door.

"Hi, Darla. Sorry to bother you this early, but…I have pressure from above to make sure you are happy with the contract and that its all signed."

"Mm, I thought I heard the doorbell ring," a sleepy Sarah announces, coming into view wearing her skimpiest of lace underwear.

"Oh, geez! So sorry! I'll be, erm…right."

I watch humorously as Sarah scoots back down the hallway towards Dante's bedroom at what must be the speed of an Olympian sprinter, all the while having one hand to cover her nether regions and the other to cover her heart shaped bottom.

"Sure, here's my contract. How come you have come here to collect it yourself? I thought I was bringing it to you later today."

"Joshua wants you moved into the apartment as soon as possible for security reasons, and it was advised as well by Max that the sooner you're settled in the better."

"That's fast, but ok. Can I get you a cup of tea or anything?" I ask, noticing how wan Eva seems to appear looking this morning.

"Tea would be lovely, thanks. Black, no sugar."

Eurgh!

"Do you have much stuff to move?"

"Not really…just clothes and some personal items. I've lived a light minimalist lifestyle all these years."

"Excellent! Well then, shall we start?"

"Pardon?" I am perplexed as to what she's trying to get at. Me…move…as in right *NOW?*

"Your things…shall we move them? We have time to do it today."

"Okay…let me just get showered and dressed and then we can get cracking." I excuse myself while Eva seems to make herself more than comfortable in Dante's apartment. Leaning against the bedroom door, my heart thunders away at a hundred miles an hour.

Somewhere in the main hub of the apartment, I hear Dante making a brief appearance to say hello before going back to the safety of his bedroom. The situation feels like it's getting more awkward by the second, so I waste no time showering. Once out of the shower and clothed, I send a quick text to Dante.

Sorry about Eva, she just…showed up. I'm moving out today.

Don't stress about it. We'll talk later, was Dante's response.

151

Say bye to Sarah for me, I texted.

Dante ends our text chat with the thumbs up emoji.

"Ok, I'm ready now."

Eva looks bemused that I just have the one duffel bag and cat carrier. "Oh…you have a *cat?!*"

"Yes, is it going to be a –"

"Let me look at him. Is it a he or a she?"

"A male. His names is Binks."

"Look at how cute he is, little Binks-Winksy," Eva speaks in a silly voice like some estranged auntie, gushing over a niece or nephew.

"Yes, he was a…rescue. My mum and I gave him a home. It's ok to take him with me, isn't it?" I ask, now feeling worried I may have missed something in the contract.

"Of *course* it's fine. I have my own cats, Welly and Boot. Welly is a white long-haired Persian and Boot is a Russian blue. They are my babies. I just love them."

Fancy that, we are both cat lovers, I consider smugly at having something in common with the "prestigious" Eva Godstone.

"Right, come along then, dear. No time like the present. We have a very busy day ahead of us. I've got to show you around the rest of Pink Club, and you will get your first real glimpse of where you're going to be dancing for our spring gala."

My stomach gets butterflies at the mention of the stage after reading in my contract that there's quite an element of danger to it.

Just before we leave, I make sure to give a swift knock on Dante's bedroom door to signal my departure. Sarah opens the door a crack and I can hear the shower running in the background.

"Bye-bye, sweetie. I am going to miss you loads," Sarah says as we give one last goodbye hug to each other.

I feel my heart breaking, knowing it will likely be some considerable time until I see my friends again. Just as I'm turning to go, Dante hurriedly rushes out of the shower in just a towel to give me a chaste kiss on the cheek before feigning kicking me out and telling me to never come back. I turn positively purple from my head to my little toe as I blush, having been so suddenly and unexpectedly up close and personal to a semi-naked Dante for the briefest of mere seconds.

Eva and I make our way down to her car, which is a very old-fashioned VW beetle. I also notice that she is wearing a plain black tracksuit with a white T-shirt under her zip-up hoodie. Binks, quite happy in his little carry case, is lying down, purring away like a little rhythmic engine.

"You were not kidding when you said you were living light. This certainly will be the easiest move I've had to organise. Bella was one for extravagance and boy did she have expensive taste. It took three moving lorries in total to shift all her stuff. Her original furniture is in there, but if you don't like it, I'm sure we can change it."

"This certainly is a lot to take in. How come you're dressed very casually today?"

"Max insists we try to dress low-key when out and about. I never have any trouble from the public, even with my pink hair being such a dead giveaway. I think I blend in well since my apartment is around Camden."

Just then my phone rings, and I can see it is my mum. "Hello, Mum…hang on a second," I say, muting my microphone. "I hate to ask this, Eva, as you've only just employed me, but can I arrange a day off? My gran passed away yesterday, and –"

"Oh my gosh! Darla, I am so very sorry! Please take the week off if need be."

"Hi, Mum…sorry, I was just confirming with my new boss. They have said it's fine and have actually very kindly granted me a week off."

My mum starts to cry on the phone, and I have to grit my teeth until our short conversation is over to prevent losing my composure in front of Eva.

"Are you ok to come to Pink Club today? Do you want to miss today's training?"

"No, thank you. My gran…she had dementia. It's with thanks to both my grandparents that I even got into dancing. Neither of them would want me to be sad or to stop living."

Eva nods in sympathy and turns on some music to cheer us both up. We pull up alongside a very fancy-looking building with huge windows and Eva grabs a ticket from a machine before driving into a private, multi-storey carpark adjacent to what must be the apartment block. She parks up in a bay closest to the entrance doors underground.

I notice that all the cars around us look very expensive. As we climb out of Eva's very out-of-place-looking pink, VW beetle, a smartly dressed couple—looking as if they are heading out for the day—greet Eva.

"Hello, Eva," the lady with dark auburn curls and Julia Robert's smile says, beaming at her.

"Hi, Sally. You and Robert heading out for a special occasion?"

"We are, indeed. Rob is taking me to see a performance of "The

Lion King" for our eleventh wedding anniversary!" Sally exclaims excitedly.

Jealousy pangs inside me, as I love stage shows and have always wanted to see "The Lion King." Then my jealousy bubble pops as I realise where I am and the job I'm about to step into.

"Have a wonderful evening, and many happy returns," Eva calls out. "Right, come on, today is all about you. I'm so excited to show you your new apartment."

"If I am living here, then how come those people know you so well?" I ask, a tad confused.

"I used to live here until Bella made a real fuss that her place of residency wasn't 'glamorous' enough so we swapped. I was fine with the move, as it is a big space for one person, and I like cosier settings."

We ride a lift to the thirteenth floor and, ironically, my apartment is also the number thirteen. *At least remembering my floor and number will be easy,* I think as we reach the front door of my new home.

"Before we go in, can I just take a second to enjoy this moment?" I ask, gently stopping Eva's hand as she raises it to open the door.

"Certainly," Eva nods.

Closing my eyes and taking a deep breath, I say a big "thank you" to the powers that be before giving the nod that I am ready. Eva opens the door, which is painted in a beautiful white colour and has a polished brass handle. With all the high-tech stuff at Pink Club, I'm amazed to see it is just a simple lock and key mechanism to gain entry into the apartment.

"Oh…my…"

"Told you it's big!"

The space is enormous! I could probably fit *two* of Dante's apartments in here. On entering the apartment, I am greeted by a large open space where a beautiful glass dining table with ten chairs around it sits in the centre. The floor has a soft white plush carpet. Off to the left is the kitchen space with plenty of room for making meals *Note to self: Learn how to cook properly.* To the right of the lounge seating area is a fabulously *huge* fireplace, and Eva demonstrates the clap-on-clap-off mechanism. Above the fireplace is a television which would be worthy of a small cinema screen.

"We have had the carpets replaced and the entire place has had a deep clean. We ditched Bella's bed and I chose a new one for the next occupant, but if you don't like it, please feel free to choose your very own," Eva happily chirps. I can barely hear her for the ringing in my ears as my anxiety climbs with my brain trying to compute just exactly where I'm going to be living now.

We walk down a corridor and Eva needs another key to unlock the bedroom. Inside, I all but fall over in shock and amazement. It is *stunning.* The décor is all very fresh and bright. There is a massive queen-sized bed with a beautiful pine coloured headboard. The bed has been made up in crisp white linen sheets and what looks to be some seriously fluffy pillows. The place oozes a simple, yet inviting, design. My new en-suite bathroom is, as you'd have guessed it to be, huge and looks like one of those expensive spa bathrooms I've seen on TV or magazines where people go to relax. I can't wait to sample the Jacuzzi!

My very own Jacuzzi…is this even real?!! I am still in unbelief of my luck and wonder if maybe I have actually fallen into a happy coma somewhere back in my *real life*.

Once the tour of my new abode is over, we head back to the kitchen area. "Anything you need for your fridge or bar, pay for it using this account number. They normally know it's us from our phone number if you call from the apartment landline, but just in case, here's the account number."

"Gosh, thank you very much." I am almost speechless.

"I'll sort your payroll out tomorrow. Do you have any social media accounts?"

"No, well…yes, but I haven't used mine in a while. Not since…erm…no, not really."

"Good, don't use them. Better yet, delete them. Your name will now be owned as a brand name attached to Pink Club, so I will organise your own PR website, social media and so on. Anything you want to post online will have to be verified first, which was stated in your contract. I hope that's ok."

"Yeah, sure. Honestly, I don't even use my own social media, so it would be much easier having someone doing it for me."

"Great. Right, let's get to Pink Club and have you acquainted with your new best friend: your stage!" There's a glint in Eva's eyes I'm beginning to recognise is a trademark for her when she's excited about something.

~ *Chapter 29* ~

Max knocks and enters Joshua's apartment where he finds him sitting and reading the newspaper.

"I have the file you requested on Darla Pebble —"

"Destroy it."

"Are you sure?"

"Yes. I don't want to pry into the woman's private life. Stella will just have to accept that she is clean and has no criminal record, which is what you've discovered, right?"

"That is true. Very well, consider it gone."

"How has she been getting on learning the ropes?" Joshua asks. This surprises both himself and Max at the genuine interest in Pink Club's new leading dance lady when he hadn't shown much—if any—interest since Mimi's death.

"From what I have seen and heard, she has been settling in very well. Eva informed me she has just moved into Bella's old apartment."

"Yes, of course, the apartment. Right, well, I'm not going out today, so you can clock off early if you like."

"Very well. Enjoy your day relaxing at home."

Good to know she's settling in well. Perhaps this new woman will be good for Pink Club after all, Joshua thinks while firing up his laptop. He prepares an email to Stella Almasi.

Dear Stella,

I am just writing to you to let you know that our new dancing lady, Darla Pebble, is completely clean and has no past or present criminal record. Max did a full background check on her; everything checks out ok. Eva has also moved her into the apartment and that all seems to have gone smoothly. I will be in touch with further updates. Let me know of any questions you may have.

Regards,

Joshua Glass.

Managing director of Pink Club

Once the email has been sent, Joshua begins to get itchy fingers and tells himself that just a quick look won't hurt. He then logs into Pink Club's security cameras and watches the staff milling about until he finds his intended target: one Darla Pebble. Shocking himself at how weird his behaviour is—and not quite sure why he's so interested in her—Joshua quickly closes his laptop and decides to head off to the gym in his apartment to clear his head and get back to the business of just managing Pink Club from afar. It has been a long time since Joshua has felt anything since his twin sister's death, but something about Darla has stirred something within him for the first time in a long time.

* * * * *

Eva told me to bring Binks along, as they even have a special pet pampering parlour here for celebrities who wish to bring their furry companions. So, I hand over my furry little friend into the safe (Eva assures me) hands of a lady called Layla, who is wearing black trousers, a white shirt, and a black waistcoat which has the *cutest* little hot pink paw prints on the top left. Binks goes willingly to her without so much as a complaint. *Traitor,* I think as I watch her carry him off.

"Ok, what shall we do first? The tour of the rest of our amazing establishment or your stage."

"Can I see the stage first?"

"Of course you can. Follow me." There is a bounce to Eva's step as we walk across the fluffy pink carpet that I've noticed runs entirely through the main body of Pink Club.

We walk some distance until she takes me through two doors clearly marked **BACK STAGE STAFF ONLY!** Once we enter through the heavy doors, I get the familiar sense and feel of backstage and it feels like home. There are wires and lighting rigs dotted about, technical equipment and other much more fun things like costume rails. Eventually, we navigate our way through to a very dark wide open circular space.

"Ok, wait here. I just have to get someone to help me," Eva says, leaving me alone a while in the darkness, which comforts me.

A dark-skinned male, who I instantly recognise as Midnight, appears, and following behind him are the rest of the dance troupe whose names I have memorised: Digit, Siren, Medley and Mixer.

"Hi. Erm…where did Eva go?" I ask, feeling very vulnerable and out of my comfort zone in the company of the men who gave me quite the frosty reception yesterday.

"Relax—you will see Eva in a moment. Follow me," Midnight instructs, and I do as I'm told.

We move further into the back of the round space where I am gently guided to a spot on the floor where there is a steel pole protruding through the basement floor. Midnight tells me to hold onto the pole, which feels cool and smooth in my hands but rougher than my pole dancer pole. "Try to relax." Midnight tells me. He reassures me that he and the rest of the gang will be here to stop me falling off the stage.

Holy shit! is all I have time to think before there is a loud bell ringing sound and then beeping noise before the floor begins to move slowly upwards. My hands move up the pole as we gently begin ascending.

"Relax. Honestly, it will be fine. Just don't let go until I tell you, ok?" Midnight says in his deep husky alpha male voice, which makes my knees go all a quiver.

Oh well; if I do end up being an exception to the safety rule and plunge to my death, at least I'll die happy, surrounded by very hunky men, I think humorously as we continue to climb.

A noise above, sounding like clicking and whirring, reverberates around us, and looking up, I can see what appears to be the floor to a room above opening up. As we reach the top, the pole vanishes as the moving floor we are on becomes flush with the floor above. It is dimly lit, but I can make out an enormous theatre in the round.

"Excuse me, Darla, but it is necessary for me to hold onto your waist to help you balance for this next part," Midnight says, being very gentlemanly about his request.

Polite and sexy. Have I just died and gone to heaven? "Sure, that's fine with me."

Midnight places his big hands on my tiny waist and then silently, as if we are floating, we rise higher and higher into the air. "How high up are we going?!" I ask, alarmed, as we now seem much higher than I'd thought we would be.

"Forty feet."

"Ok, yeah, that's what I was told. It sure does seem a lot higher, though. How will people see us dancing up here? I know it's in the round, but what about the people at the back of the seating rows?"

"That big cinema screen there will be ensuring everyone can see you up close and personal."

I look around then for Eva and see her comfortably sitting in one of the pink velvet fold-up chairs.

"How's our girl doing up there, Midnight?" Eva asks through what I notice is a small mic that Midnight wears in his ear.

"She's doing good," he responds happily.

"Ok, let's go for a walk now." Midnight removes his hands from my waist and walks to my left while taking hold of my hand. The other guys take up designated spots on the stage.

As my confidence builds, I can see the stage has been made to look like a Celtic cross, which is pink with a black outline. Midnight's calm demeanour begins to rub off on me and I find I become more and more relaxed. He walks me to the middle and encourages me to do a small twirl while still having firm hold of my hand.

"Ok, I think that will do for today. Your training will begin more rigorously in the coming weeks," Midnight informs me gruffly.

The other dancers remain silent, and I wonder if they will ever soften towards me. Midnight then gives the command to Eva to begin lowering the stage, and soon we are back down into the vast open circular void. The dancers saunter off, but Midnight waits with me until Eva comes to meet us.

"Don't worry about the other guys. They are still a bit sore since one of our crew…well, he –"

"Died?! He fell off the stage?!" I say interrupting Midnight with my presumption someone has died, feeling shocked how I had been led to believe nothing like this had happened.

"Bella was high maintenance and at times extremely volatile. During a routine rehearsal, Fixer, our youngest dance guard, noticed she was off balance. When he went to prevent her from toppling— which he was trained to do—she swung her arm out, shoving him back. The momentum was enough to push him off the edge. He didn't die, but the force of impact on landing shattered his pelvis and broke his back, so he now gets about in a wheelchair."

"Jesus! Thank God he didn't die! I'm so sorry. I hope the guys don't think that –"

"It is a trust issue, and trust takes time. Don't worry; I'm sure they will come around. You seem…nice."

However kind Midnight's words are, they do not fill me with much reassurance. Bella put a man in the hospital and ruined his life, and she was a professional, well-qualified dancer! I'm basically a novice compared to someone like her. What if I knock someone off the stage and they don't just end up with broken bones?

"How was that? Did you have fun up there?" Eva interrupts my worried thoughts as she comes into view with a beaming smile.

Midnight and the other dancers have disappeared, and after what Midnight just told me, my previous euphoria has now been replaced with dread and uncertainty.

"Yeah, it was great up there, it's just…well, Midnight told me about the *incident* with another one of your dancers, Fixer."

"Oh, he did, did he?" Eva's smile vanishes and it seems like storm clouds are brewing in her eyes.

"Max! Get me Midnight and the rest of the team back to my office right NOW!"

I blanch when I hear how angry Eva is. If the guys were not too sure about me, they sure as eggs is eggs are going to hate my guts now for pissing Eva off and getting them into trouble.

Shit! "It's no big deal, really!" I try in vain to deter Eva from giving the men a dressing down but to no avail.

We seem to reach her office in record time. Mind you, with the speed she had been walking, I almost found myself having to jog at times just to keep up. How she managed just such a speed in kitten heels on this bouncy carpet is a mystery—possibly fuelled along by rage and adrenaline I wonder.

"The guys are already inside," Max informs Eva as we enter.

"Thanks, Max."

Once we are both inside, Eva shuts the door, taking a deep breath to compose herself before royally ripping into all of them. And when I say *royally ripping into them,* I mean it. Eventually, she finishes her mini tirade about how I am to be treated with the upmost respect, that I am not Bella Fitzroy, and how any further incidents will conclude in them receiving an instant dismissal.

"Now, I would like you to apologise to our newest star performer and be nothing else but kind and courteous to her. Do I make myself clear?"

The men glare at me through seemingly gritted teeth, saying a mumbled 'sorry' before Eva allows them to leave.

"To be fair to Midnight, Eva, he was very nice to me up on the stage. He was the one assuring me that the guys will warm up to me."

"Even so, I will not be having some of our highest paying staff members here behaving so appallingly. Now about Fixer. As you are well aware now—as are most of the dancing and performing arts world—of the incident…Bella had a very bad drug addiction to cocaine. This was the defining factor to Fixer's accident and injuries, but the truth is that any of you could fall at any time up there. The difference is the risk. If you're all compos mentis, then the chance of your falling is no different to that of horse riding, for example. As a result of Fixer's accident, we now have an inflatable floor, so should anyone fall off there, they bypass a sensor which triggers the equivalent of a car airbag, which comes up from under the floor. I hope that reassures you that it's just the illusion of danger, because it is, in fact, quite safe."

"I'm glad to hear about the safety feature with the floor. That really has given me peace of mind."

"Good. Well, now that we sorted this little issue with your stubborn safety dance team, let's introduce you to the rest of Pink Club and the pièce de ré·sis·tance: your dressing room. How are you feeling? Do you need a break before we do more of your tour? I am concerned you have just lost your grandmother and –"

165

"The tour has been a much-needed distraction. I'm fine; please lead on," I say honestly, as it really has helped take mind off grans passing to have something to enjoyable to do. She would have loved this place and I imagine her in spirit following us around.

~ *Chapter 30* ~

Stella Almasi is busily topping up her tan on Bondi beach. Her and her husband Mohammad's private marquee shields them from the rest of the general public. Stella is alone on the beach, however, as her estranged husband has chosen to stay in the luxury holiday apartment that they have rented for three months. Powering up her laptop, Stella is pleased to see an email with an update from Joshua. Her loins immediately stir to life, remembering their short intense affair between the sheets. But knowing she is still not forgiven for taking Pink Club from under him and Mimi *illegally,* Stella's body soon cools at recalling just how upset and angry Joshua was. She couldn't see the harm—it was only *her* name that was attached to Pink Club as the owner and the fact she funded everything. The complete running and design of Pink Club had been handed over completely to the twins. She justifies that she only made Joshua guarantor as a failsafe in case he didn't go along with her plan, and for her it looked like a good call, as her actions could have left her deeply embarrassed and out of pocket by having to go through a court case. As it stood, though, she'd managed with her lawyers to wrangle enough red tape that made Joshua and Mimi back down. They wouldn't have been able to afford the legal costs that they would need in order to beat someone like Stella in court.

Reading the email, Stella is pleased to see that the new dancer has no criminal record. A photograph is included in the email and Stella finds the new dancer is really rather quite pretty. A little green monster stirs within her, but she soon quashes it. Fingers at the ready, Stella forms her reply.

Dear Joshua,

It pleases me greatly to know that our new leading dance lady sounds as pure as the driven snow. All the same, I would like a drug test run on her as soon as possible. We can't be too careful after what happened to Bella. Please arrange a bouquet of flowers and some bubbly for her as a welcome gift from myself, as I am not currently there in person. Mo and I are in Australia until Feb.

Keep me posted on her training.

Warmest Wishes,

Stella. XX

* * * * *

Eva and I continue my tour of Pink Club, beginning with a room called Fairy Fantasy. The dark brown wooden doors are made to look like the trunk of a tree, and there are gemstones imbedded into the faux bark of the wood. An intricate metallic vine design covers the doors in greens and golds.

"Ok, so this has to be one of my absolute favourite rooms which Mimi invented, designed and decorated. You will need your shoes off again before we go in," Eva says, and we both slip our footwear off our feet.

On entry into The Fairy Fantasy room, I'm immediately aware of the feeling of grass beneath my feet. Looking down, I see that there is, in fact, real grass! The entire room is more like an indoor woodland. There are real trees, picnic tables, and at the far end of the space a really cute stage area with purple sparkly curtains, and a floor made to look like a big, flat, round tree stump. From the ceiling there are fairy lanterns and a 3D lighting device (a bit like a disco ball but with laser technology), which makes fairy shapes dance along the forest wall. Off to the left I can see an authentic looking gypsy caravan, and I'm told by Eva that they use the room a lot for guests who want to have a more *magical* experience as a form of entertainment. Guests can request to have a Tarot reading by Pink Club's own in-house fortune teller named "Silvia Moon," enjoy an intimate setting for those who have eclectic tastes in alternative music artists, or just enjoy a quiet night in of psychic mediumship, as Pink Club allows well known celebrity psychics such as Katie Helliwel through its doors to entertain people of a more spiritual nature.

I follow Eva along a path made of rustic flagstones to where a bar is situated. The bar has been made to look like it's imbedded inside a real tree. Green foliage hangs down the front of the bar, and the stools have been designed to look like flat purple topped mushrooms. Plinky plonky music plays out of a speaker as a man dressed in dark purple attire asks Eva and I if we would like something to drink.

"Sorry, Tibalt, maybe another day. I've got to show our new leading dancer here the rest of the amazing spaces we have," Eva tells the smartly dressed man in purple.

"Well, I look forward to serving you on another day then, Eva and..."

"Oh, sorry, how rude of me. This is Darla," Eva says, and I pick up on a slight tinge of embarrassment lacing her voice.

"It is a pleasure to meet you, Darla. Here is my card. I like to do some freelancing mixology when off duty here, so if you ever need some help with a party or whatnot, I'm your guy," Tibalt says with a wink as Eva speedily steers me away from the bar.

"Th-thank you. I'll certainly keep you in mind," I call over my shoulder as Eva chastens our exit out of The Fairy Fantasy room.

Once we are back outside, it takes my eyes a while to adjust to the heady pink lighting again. Pink Club has their own cinema room which is exactly what it says it is: a cinema. A lot of stars do private premieres of their movies here, which is when Eva says I will definitely need my autograph book.

Then there is the 1920's ballroom called The Green Dragon where performances of classic dance shows from that era are held, such as the very famous and old style of tea dances. Hanging from the ceiling are massive crystal chandeliers that were bought at an auction from a real 1920's ballroom that had long since been decommissioned. The floor is made of polished walnut wood, indoor Palm trees are dotted about, and the décor is completely that of the 1920's. The bar is labelled as a Cuban cocktail bar in bright neon lighting and taking centre stage is a grand piano. My grandparents would have loved this room and the thought threatens to overwhelm me.

"Where did the name come from?"

"Our research showed us that the chandeliers had come from an old hotel called The Green Dragon, so to pay homage to all the generations that would have danced under these very same chandeliers, we decided to name this room after the hotel."

Swiftly, we move onto the second to last room called Pretty Kitty, a room I know Binks would just love; it is a pet-friendly parlour. The room is decorated to look like a Chinese themed animal-friendly café come library. All pets brought onto the premises have to show they have a passport and have been cleared of any diseases or illnesses. Pink Club even has their own on-site vet and animal carers for guests who wish to have a night of fun while their pets are pampered in the process. A lot of puppies and kittens get booked into their pet sitting service, as owners don't like leaving their young fur babies behind. Eva says I can bring Binks here whenever I like, but I think if I ever bought him here, he'd get too spoilt and grow a serious cat attitude.

The café sells little intricately designed cakes and pastries, and the drink menu is beautifully artistic. There are amazing sundaes and hot chocolates among their stylish coffees and tea that they serve. With all the books they have to read in here as well, I already know that I shall be spending a lot of time in this room.

The last room I'm taken to is called Freaky Frankenstein, used most popularly for Halloween functions and is very enticing for guests who like to follow a more gothic way of life. There's a faux faraday cage and within it lies the bar area. A big green, mean-looking Frankenstein head hangs from the ceiling. The eating area takes up the first and second floors, and spooky music filters out across the room from hidden speakers. The first-floor area can be adapted to form a

171

dance floor for when they have musicians coming to play and advertise their new albums.

Staff dressed in black and white waiter and waitressing uniforms are preparing the space for use, which is when a chef clocks us and tells us to 'hang fire' before we leave. He soon returns with a tray of baked goodies: double chocolate chip muffins with lime green coloured icing and little edible Frankenstein toppers, and warm bleeding oat cookies filled with strawberry jam.

"What do you think of my latest creations?" the chef asks Eva theatrically. I notice he has a French accent.

"Bloody lovely," Eva responds through a mouthful of bleeding oat cookie.

"Yes, well, at £1,200 a cake and cookie, I'd hope they were…how do you say…*bloody lovely?* Who is your beautiful, flaxen-haired friend, Ma Cherie?"

Holy shit! £1,200 for a sodding cookie or muffin! What are they laced with, liquid gold?! I've seen extravagant food online of items such as a pizza costing half a million dollars, but actually holding the space with such a chef seemed next level nuts. What's happened to my life?

"I see you've used only the best ingredients for our well-paying guests this evening. This is Darla, our newest star dancer taking place of—you know…Bella."

"Ahh, so this is the young woman everyone has been busily chatting about. Well, Darla, my name is Maurice, and if you ever need anything, I know how to cook more than just themed party cakes." Maurice winks at me and I blush a little.

"Thanks, I will keep that in mind. My birthday is the first of

January…maybe you could bake me a cake?" I cheekily reply and instantly regret it, thinking of how rude I must have just sounded. "So sorry…how rude of me…"

"Your *BIRTHDAY*?! On the first, you say? How *wonderful*! New Year's Day! And this will be your *first* birthday here with us. It would be an honour for me to make you a birthday cake!" Maurice exclaimed excitedly, grinning widely.

"Your birthday is New Year's *DAY*! How did I miss this? I think I have a brilliant idea brewing. Seeing as we have every room fully booked during New Year's, this event would really help pimp your profile within our celebrity community here at Pink Club. Yes! We will give all focus to you on your *birthday,* and as the clock strikes midnight on New Year's Eve, you will perform a small routine to dance in the new year with everybody. Your big debut of course won't be going ahead until we have our annual spring gala in March—but we can start the ball rolling to get people interested in our new leading lady earlier just to tease our loyal customers of what's to come. Oh, this is going to be such fun!" Eva says, wandering away from where Maurice and I stand, muttering things to herself. I can only watch on in silent horror as the cogs appear to be whirring away inside Eva's mind and all I can think to myself is *shitballs*.

"Actually, would you mind if we *didn't* let everyone know it is my birthday New Year's Day?" I say, which halts Eva in her full flow babble mode with herself.

"Nonsense! The opportunity is way too good to let go of for publicity. This will give our guests all the confidence they need to have faith restored in us that we do, in fact, have a brand-new performer for the spring gala, which would also help cool down my email inbox and voicemail. Then finally people will start gossiping about something else other than Bella *bloody* Fitzroy! I love it when a plan comes together. For surely once everyone watches you dancing, tongues are sure to wag. This is great news, indeed!" Eva exclaims, doing a gleeful little solitary celebratory clap right in front of me.

My stomach and heart sink. Suddenly, I feel like a puppet on strings and this deeply unnerves me. It appears I really have become like a piece of property and the notion makes me wince as I feel my freedom flitting away.

Accepting defeat that I have no say, I take a pew on one of the chairs laid out for the event tonight while Eva and Maurice start to excitedly jabber about cake ideas. Oh, how I wish Frankenstein were real right about now so he could mash me into oblivion.

~ *Chapter 31* ~

All too soon it is the third of December, the day of my grandmother's funeral. On route to the cemetery, I see shop windows and houses starting to don their Christmas lights and decorations, but there is nothing about the cheerful scenes that can lift my heavy-hearted mood.

I decide to focus on what's been going well for me on the car ride over. My training on the raised stage has been smooth so far, and the guys have been warming to me. However, now that I've been given the week off from rehearsing on stage at Pink Club, I worry my newfound skills will slip. Although I tried to plead with Eva that it wasn't necessary, she told me it wasn't up to her—her big boss had the final say and she had insisted I have the week off. The big boss has also sent me a second lot of flowers. Well, this time it was a planter, actually. The accompanying card reads:

Darla,

I am so sorry to hear of your grandmother's passing. Please accept this planter as a token of my condolences.

Stella x

The kiss at the end unsettles me—far too over-familiar and I get a strong sense to watch my back where this Stella woman is concerned.

Mum and John have finally moved out of the old pokey apartment I used to share with her and into a much more respectable two up/two down council house. Mum received the long-awaited compensation money from the devastating fire of our old council apartment. All residents got a pay-out because of the mistakes made from shoddy workmanship by unqualified cowboy builders. In their wisdom, the council had decided to put cladding around our building to make it look less offensive to the rich, and as a result of this so-called work, a small fire started in one apartment and rapidly ripped through the rest.

Living where I am now, I can't really resent my mum splashing all the money on her and John, but she doesn't know my change in circumstances, and when I think about that it does piss me off and sting a bit. I choose not to focus on it.

My mind wanders to thoughts of my old life, the past living and working arrangements to then memories of my grandparents. A ping on my phone lets me know I've received my first payment paid into my bank account from Pink Club. Logging on, I wait for my balance to show up and almost knock myself unconscious on the kitchen sideboard as I see the amount. £15,000! *Are you frickin kidding me!* My mind now whirs and funny dots swim in my vision. Feeling as if I am having the mother of all hot flushes, it takes me a few minutes to get my head together as I check and re-check and check again at the amount.

"Oh my God! They've made a mistake!" I cry, beginning to panic as I dial Eva's number.

"Hi, Darla, are you ok? I know it is your gran's funeral today –"

"Yes, erm, hi…no, it's not anything to with my gran's funeral. It's just…I think payroll made a mistake," I cut Eva off, my mind now racing.

"Really? Let me just check the system…one minute."

"Ok."

"No, everything checks out our end. Fifteen thousand pounds has been deposited to your account successfully."

"Fifteen…thousand…" I mumble quietly.

"Are you still there, Darla?"

I wake from my dazed reverie. "Yes, I just…well, it's a lot of money."

"Trust me, that's nothing to what you'll be earning once you're wowing the crowds."

"How much—just out of interest—am I going to be earning?"

"Six figures. Sorry I didn't explain to you what your exact wages would be. I forget you come from humble beginnings."

"It sure is a lot of dough!" I say, suddenly feeling as if I want to strip naked and dive into an ice-bath.

"Mm, yes. I admit for myself my designer walk-in wardrobe is one of the loves in my life. Right, well, I have to run, but I hope your grandmother's funeral service goes as well as it can and see you back here in a week," Eva says before disconnecting our call.

Looking at my phone, I can see it is, indeed, almost time to meet my mum and John for Gran's funeral service. I'm already dressed in my chosen outfit. My gran loved sunflowers, so I've chosen to wear a black hat designed with sunflowers, a black, figure-hugging dress that

I found on sale. It cost £50 and was much more than I would usually spend on clothes for myself. Mum and I had relied heavily on the charity of others for years. At the time of purchasing the dress, I thought I had just £350 in the bank. It tickles me, as I'd been painstakingly choosing between a £20 dress and the now £50 dress I wore, while all the time totally unaware of the money I'd just received from Pink Club. My gran, I'm sure, would have also been amused. We had a similar sense of humour.

I added a lemon-yellow sash to brighten the outfit, along with my pastel yellow kitten heels (taking a leaf out of Eva's book on fancy footwear), and sheer black tights finish my look. It is a beautiful sunny day but jolly cold, so I wear my smart black raincoat and take a brolly with me just in case.

Binks has settled into our new home very nicely (no surprise there, spoilt little furball that he is). En-route to meeting Mum and John, I make a quick online order for a luxury cat tower for Binks and some cat toys. I also start looking for some new clothes and things to begin to fill the apartment with such as bookshelves to help fill the space and make it appear more homely. My thoughts ruminate of just how out of my depth I am with decorating, so I make a mental note to check out interior designers later.

Eva left me some useful numbers, and among them is the number for a private taxi firm Pink Club employees are encouraged to use. I only have to wait five minutes for the taxi to show up. The driver very kindly gets out to open the door for me. Once he has the coordinates for the crematorium, we make our way. Thoughts of my grandmother's happy smiling face come to the forefront of my mind, and I battle to keep the tears at bay.

As my driver, Trevor, helps me back out of the car, he hands me his own personal card and tells me to call him, should I require a lift in the future, and if he's available he will come and collect me. Trevor is a nice man and I'm very thankful for the gesture, as it has always been a fear of mine to get taxis by myself.

Once I'm inside the crematorium, my mum comes galloping over to me and gives me just the biggest of hugs. "Ok, can't breathe," I mumble, gently tapping my mum on her arm.

"I'm just so glad that you're here," my mum whispers through a fresh bout of tears.

"Come on, let's go and take a pew." John gently guides my mum to our seats at the front.

Looking around, I see some ladies, who I assume are my grandmother's friends, dotted about in other chairs. They give bowing nods of condolence before the vicar begins his sermon.

At the end of the service, I am absolutely ruined. My hand has gone numb from where my mother's grabbed hold of it for grim death. John has arranged a wake in the pub across from the crematorium. It has the classic London pub feel and there is a lovely spread of finger sandwiches and cakes on display as we enter.

My grandmother's friends come and say a solemn hello, and I welcome the distraction from my grief that chatting with them brings with it. They tell me amazing stories about my grandmother and what they used to get up to as children and teenagers.

I notice my mother has hidden herself away in a far corner of the pub and is picking at the food. John can do nothing to console her. I watch as he gets up and approaches to where I am now standing with two of gran's friends, Nora and Joan. They had all been in the same house with my grandmother when they were all evacuated during WWII, and the trio became fast friends and stayed that way right up until my gran's death.

"Darla, I think I'm going to take your mum home. She's not good."

"Ok, thank you, John. I'll see if I can pop by later, perhaps?"

"Maybe tomorrow would be better. Your mum and I are going on holiday in a few days with some of the inheritance money your gran left her. I think the break will do her some good."

"Oh, really? Where are you going?" I am finding it hard to compose myself as it's the first I've heard of any would-be inheritance.

"She booked a last-minute deal to Spain."

"Spain??" I exclaim, feeling as if someone or something is now squeezing my heart. That was the one place I shared so many happy holiday memories with my grandparents. "Well, have a nice time, both of you. I think its best you take her home now." I turn away from John to continue my conversation with Nora and Joan, my stomach in knots and my heart a shattered mess.

Mum has ALL the money? But Gran and Grandad always knew how hairbrained she was with financial things. Something doesn't feel right. I need to look deeper at this situation.

~ *Chapter 32* ~

Once back at home, I can't get thoughts out of my head that something is amiss regarding money left by my grandmother. Putting on my detective noggin, I decide to give gran's old care home a ring.

"Hello, Darla," Martha greets once she comes on the line. I had requested her specifically to speak to when reception answered.

"Hi, Martha —"

"I am so sorry about your grandmother," she interrupts.

"Thank you. The service was really lovely. I wonder, Martha, if you wouldn't be able to tell me if my mother ever went to visit my gran, would you?"

"Ah…yes…not very often but she did visit with a gentleman—a lawyer, I think—if memory serves me. I hope everything is ok…"

My stomach reels. "Oh yes. I forgot about the lawyer visit. My grandmother was always a stickler for getting her affairs in order. She was a whizz at math, you know. Thanks so much for your help, Martha."

"Is there anything else I can help you with?"

"No, thank you. Oh, but I would like to make a £1,000 donation to the care home."

"Wow—that's jolly kind of you!"

"My gran would have wanted to give something back; that's just the kind of woman she was."

As we hang up the phone, my blood is boiling with rage. I know exactly what my mother's little *visits* will have meant, but until I know for sure, and can confront her face to face, I don't think I can begin to heal from this level of betrayal.

Calling my mum and John's new number, I decide to play it cool and arrange to see them both the next day. John answers the phone and in the background my mother is yelling as she says, "I can't BELIEVE you told her about the holiday!"

"Of course, we would love to see you tomorrow. Your mum's actually gone down for a sleep. Shall we say noon tomorrow then?" John's voice is tense.

Liar, I think, knowing full well I had just heard my mum in the background. "Yes, noon sounds good for me. I shall see you then."

"Ok, Darla, see you tomorrow," John says hurriedly. I can now hear more of an edge to his voice as sounds of smashing come through the phone mic.

By the end of the short phone call, I feel drained. My eyes feel as if they have cried themselves dry, and just as I am about to take a bath and do not much else for the rest of the day, there is a knock on my door. I can see its Eva through the peephole. Sighing, I unlock the door and am taken aback to see not just Eva but also Dante, Sarah, Octavia, Midnight, Digit, Mixer, Medley and Siren!

"Sorry to arrive uninvited, but we thought you might like some company," Eva greets rather sheepishly.

A wide grin spreads across my face as I go to hug my best friends, Dante and Sarah.

"We brought plenty of bubbly with us." Sarah holds up a bottle pink champagne.

"Excellent! Let me just go and freshen up. Make yourselves at home. I'll be right back."

Quickly dashing down the hallway to my bedroom, I think of how good it feels to see my friends after such a shitty day, and I also love the fact that my safeguarding dance team are here too. My dance training has already started, but I haven't yet been able to get to know any of the staff at Pink Club off the clock properly. Now, given this opportunity, I don't really want to ruin it by behaving like a sad clown.

Returning to the small party, I see that the music is playing Shakira's "Wherever, Whenever" and the bubbly is flowing.

"Where did the...food come from?" I ask amazed to see a fine spread of finger sandwiches and other nibbly bits, both sweet and savoury, for the second time today. However, now I have more of an appetite.

"Pink Club has connections to some of the best caterers around," Eva answers, handing me a glass of pink bubbles.

Of course it does—silly me, I think as Octavia hands me a plate of nibbles consisting of mini pizzas, sausage rolls and fruit cocktail sticks with a cube of cheese, cherry and grape.

Dante and Sarah are dancing away now to "Gettin' Jiggy With It" and, for once, I realise I don't feel jealous of them anymore—just happy.

As we all begin to unwind more with the alcohol and good music, Eva breaks out the game Twister she had brought with her as a team building/ice breaking exercise. I blush a deep shade of scarlet when I have to place my arms between Midnight's legs, unbalancing him and causing him to fall over. We all fall about laughing and it feels so good to let my hair down for the first time in what feels like has been an eternity.

Too soon, though, it's getting on for three in the morning and time for everyone to go home. As I say my goodbyes, the air feels well and truly cleared with Midnight, Digit, Mixer, Medley and Siren, especially seeing as they ALL give me a kiss on the cheek and hug before leaving. Sarah and Dante said that now they have my new address, they will be able to pop over more frequently. I also hear that Sarah has moved in with Dante permanently. I'm really happy for them. Eva and Octavia help me to clear up before they go to head out, and by the time they leave, I feel much better.

"Right *now,* a bath and then a good night...er, morning's sleep," I tell Binks as I head off towards my bedroom. When my head hits one of my comfortable cloud-like pillows, the world falls away and I'm asleep within minutes.

* * * * *

"I'm sorry Rumer...I can't do this anymore. Your mood swings...they're just crazy!"

"Don't say that! Don't you DARE say that I am CRAZY!" Rumer spits back at John with a wild, unrecognisable look in her eyes.

John picks up his suitcase, knowing that he can't reason with

Rumer in this state. "I'll call you in a few days when the air has cleared," is the last thing John says before placing his fedora hat upon his head, and armed with passport in hand, steps out of the apartment.

* * * * *

Looking at my bedside clock I see it's already 10:30 in the morning. Binks is busily meowing and purring away at me, keen to have his breakfast, no doubt.

"Ok, I'm going, I'm going," I say, sleepily yawning and stretching.

Then, on Binks's cat command, I get out of bed. My head doesn't feel too bad, considering the amount of pink bubbles I ingested just a few hours ago. Pouring cat biscuits in the shapes of little fishes and fresh water into Binks's bowls, I then think of what I might have for breakfast. I decide to make myself a full English with fried sausages, scrambled eggs, cooked tomatoes, bacon and toast.

"This is the life, aye Binks?" I prop my feet up on an ottoman and take a nice bite out of my toast from my plate of yummy sustenance and pop on the TV.

"The Sound of Music" is on, which is one of my favourites. My grandparents first showed the movie to me when I had just started dancing lessons at Busy Bee's. I can remember us all sitting together one Sunday afternoon with Mum, after we had just devoured one of my grandmother's famous roast lunches. It was a really lovely memory, and the warm fuzzy feeling makes me feel as if my grandparents are with me now.

~ *Chapter 33* ~

Calling Eva, I ask permission to get back to training as soon as tomorrow. I'm happy to hear she's only too pleased to have me back sooner, and once she clears it with the head boss, I get ready to meet my mum and John.

The earlier anger I had at my mother has ebbed away after some sleep, and I realise it really doesn't matter what she does or doesn't do with whatever money my grandmother had left behind because I am beginning my dream dancing job and she will never be any the wiser…at least, not if I have anything to say about it.

Once showered and dressed, I make my way down to the apartment block carpark where Trevor picks me up. "Good morning, Darla. Where are we going today?" Trevor greets cheerily.

"Number twenty-one, Flagstone Street, please," I reel off my mum and John's new home address.

"Right you are then."

As we set off, Trevor happily jabbers away, and even though I'm not keen for conversation, I do like the needed distraction for what might be about to happen when I see my mum. Do I confront her and have it out with her, or do I let sleeping dogs lie?

"Here we are—number twenty-one. That'll be £8.53, please."

Before I'm even out of the taxi, I'm horrified to see my mum running towards me, arms stretched out wide. She looks wild and I hurriedly try to get away from Trevor and his taxi so that he doesn't know this crazy-haired, tear-streaked woman running half naked in her silk nightie (lady of the night-esque) is anything to do with me. I'm not fast enough, though, and just as I step out onto the pavement, she is on me like some deranged baboon. Her hair is sticking out at all angles and her black roots shout at her ginger ends. It is then I notice she's fallen out of the nightie, and I notice Trevor's face looks momentarily stunned—his eyes out on stalks—before driving away at speed.

"Come on, let's get inside. It's freezing out here," I say, trying to sprint away. However, I am unable to, as my mother's death grip makes our journey back into her apartment painfully slow. We cross the communal lawn at a snail's pace while all the neighbours and passers-by just stand gawping at the pair of us.

Once we reach the apartment complex, we have to wait for what seems an eternity for someone to buzz us in. John is nowhere to be seen, and putting two and two together, I'm guessing he has left her in the lurch.

Finally gaining entry inside, I'm thankful to see mum's new place is on the ground floor. I hear a door shut and footsteps approaching from another apartment above, and—not wanting them to see us—I ask my mum if she has a key.

"Oh, *nooooo*," she wails into my ear, making me wince. "I left it *insiiiiide*. We're locked *ouuuuuut*."

The person I'd heard from above comes down the stairs and approaches us. Thinking fast, I take my coat off and wrap it around my mother, whose boobies I'm glad to see are now back under the nightie.

"I see you have locked yourselves out. Barry, the caretaker, is in his office, and he should be able to help you gain entry. I'm forever doing this myself," the kindly gentleman says.

"Thank you. Where can I find him?"

"I have his number, actually. Let me call him over and then he can help you."

I feel as if I could kiss this man—even with his bad halitosis and nicotine-stained fingers. Ok, maybe not kiss but definitely shake hands with.

Barry soon arrives like a knight riding in on his big white horse, although a far cry from Richard Gere. I'm just relieved to see someone has come to our rescue, as other residents have now popped their heads out to have a nose.

We eventually regain entry into Mum's property because Barry has a universal key for emergency use much like the one we have here.

"There we go. Maybe your mum should get another key cut just in case she does it again," Barry says, looking me up and down, which makes me feel queasy.

Once he is gone, I first breathe a sigh of relief before ordering my mum to take a nice hot shower and dress more appropriately. She does as she's told with not much fuss, and I get to work finding my way around. The place is small, but more spacious than the old apartment. Some utility bills sit on the side, and as tempting as it is for me to take

188

a closer look, I tear myself away, busying myself to make tea for Mum.

I wait in the lounge area, which has two small coffee-coloured corduroy sofas, a coffee table and big screen TV. I try to distract myself from the elephant in the room that will not leave.

"Thank you for the tea, my sweet girl," my mum says, wearing a much more respectable pair of pale blue jeans and white polar neck jumper. Her eyes are sunken with great big dark rims underneath, and although she smiles at me as she sits down, her smile doesn't reach her eyes.

"Right, come on. Are we, or are we not, Pebble women?! We cry over no man. Now come along, we are going out!" I exclaim, putting my teacup down.

"Where are we going?" my mum asks, speedily sipping at her tea.

"You owe me a trip to the cinema, *remember?*"

"Do you mind if we give it a miss today? I'm just feeling –"

"Nope! Come on, we're going. Get your coat; I'll wait outside. We are NOT doing the pity my poor feet parade." I stand up and walk out before my mother can argue with me, and once she steps outside, I link my arm through hers and we head off in the direction of the town centre.

* * * * *

"Flossy and Bonce" was just as lovely as I thought it would be. There were some really funny bits in the animation as well, which had Mum and I rolling about laughing. It was good to see her laughing again. Once the film finished, we decide to head off to Angel Cake for some sustenance.

"Well, if it ain't Miss D as I live and breathe," a familiar voice announces as they pass by.

"Oh my God…BONNIE?!" We give each other a bear hug. "Sorry, Bonnie, this is my mum, Rumer."

"Hi, lovely to meet you." Bonnie gives Mum a firm handshake.

"Yes, erm…lovely to meet you," I hear my mum say as she's taking in Bonnie's choice of extravagant outfits for the day. Bonnie is wearing chrome silver flared trousers, sparkly gold platform shoes, and a tiny hot green crop top under a plain white denim jacket. I wonder how she hasn't turned into a statue with it being freezing cold.

"What happened to you, girl? We all miss you back at Luci's."

"I got a new job," I answer quickly before mouthing to her, *talk to you about it later* before doing an imaginary zip line across my mouth.

"Well, congratulations, babe. I look forward to hearing all about it *soon*."

"Sure thing, Bonnie. Ciao, ciao."

"Ciao, ciao darlin'," she waves as we part ways.

"She seems…*lovely*," my mum says, not hiding her sarcasm well.

I just smile at her as we head on towards Angel Cake. The familiar smells of coffee, hot chocolate and cinnamon roll over us as we enter my little slice of heaven on earth.

"Darla!" Vera cries, coming over hurriedly to give me a hug.

"Hello, stranger. So sorry I haven't been here for a while. Oh—I see you have a new staff member," I say as she takes mine and Mum's coats to hang up.

"Yes, this is Katia; she's from Romania. Very nice girl, speaks fluent English. Moved here to become a teacher—goodness me, this must be your lovely mother I've heard so much about! The resemblance is uncanny. You sure are your mother's daughter."

"Thank you." A fresh batch of tears are already rimming my mother's eyes as she responds.

"Right, well, you go and grab a table and I'll send Katia right over."

Vera leaves us, and we make our way to a table by one of the large windows that looks out onto the road where cars and people busily go about their daily business.

"Hello, ladies. Are you ready to order yet, or do you need more time?" Katia greets brightly. She has pale skin and hair as black as a raven's wings with the most piercing blue eyes.

"We'll have two gingerbread lattes. Also, may we have a mixed platter of finger sandwiches, please?" I order for both Mum and me.

"Certainly." Katia heads off to put the order in and Mum grabs my hands from across the table with tears in her eyes again.

"You seem to make friends so easily, and I…I have no friends. Thank God I have you, otherwise I don't know what I'd do." Mum's eyes shine with fresh tears as she says this to me.

My stomach plummets, hearing Mum talk like this. There is no way I can leave her alone in this state, but what can I do? Eva already made it very clear I wasn't to tell my mum about my new job role working for Pink Club. This situation has put me into such a terrible bind.

"Won't you move back in with your old mum –"

"I'm sorry, Mum," I interrupt. "But no…I can't drop everything to—look, you ran off with John what's-his-face at the drop of a hat, took all of Gran's money without giving me a second thought, and don't you dare try to make excuses for that; I already spoke to the care home who confirmed your little visits to see her with your solicitor. Look, I think it's time we gave each other breathing space. I've lost my appetite now..."

"Oh, please don't go!" Mum cries, grabbing my arm as I stand up to leave. "You are right...about everything. Look, let's just enjoy this time together, ok? Then whatever you need, space...time...I'll do whatever you need, but just please don't leave me."

Seeing my mother's unravelled response, I sit back down. "I'm not leaving, Mum; I just want time to myself to do what I want for a change."

"That's exactly how it should be! If space is what you need, then it's what you'll have."

"I love you, Mum, and I promise to be in regular contact, but with my new job I'm going to be really busy –"

"Oh, yes—your new job! How is it going, by the way? And...where did you say you worked again?"

I begin to panic, thinking of a cover story quickly. "It's in the clause of my contract that I'm not allowed to discuss it with anyone...sorry."

My mother looks crestfallen with my response, and I feel bad about keeping this secret, seeing as Dante and Sarah know, but they've signed contracts to keep quiet and know how to keep their mouths shut, whereas my mother doesn't. The whole world would know I danced for Pink Club if I told her.

"What's this?" I ask curiously as Mum pushes a blank envelope in my direction.

"Don't open it—at least not here. Wait until you get home."

I slip the envelope into my bag as we finish the rest of our finger sandwiches and gingerbread latte's. Later, arriving back at Mum's apartment, I make sure she is settled before making my way back home. I already checked what was in the envelope in Mum's bathroom before leaving: it is a cheque for money my grandmother had left. I rip it in half and place it back inside the envelope with a quick note on the front saying, **"You need this more than me. I love you. Enjoy your holiday to Spain—just please, no boyfriends, at least for a while." XX**

As my mum closes her apartment door, and I hear her walk away, I slip the envelope under the door.

~ *Chapter 34* ~

It feels good to be back at Pink Club, throwing myself back into my dance training. It's exactly where I need to be.

"Right. Today, lovely Darla, you will be practicing aerial skills on silk ropes," Midnight announces, clasping his hands together before rubbing them vigorously, a wicked smile spreading across his face as we stand on the stage together.

I'd wondered what the two long pieces of silk rope hanging from the cross section of the raised stage were for, but the mystery was now revealed. Midnight leaps off the stage towards one of them, grabs a firm hold of the rope to swing wide, and then somehow ends up hanging upside down before flipping himself upright again and swinging back to the stage. Medley, who was standing stoically nearby, helps to draw him back onto the platform, a very focused look in his eyes, saying nothing.

"I…I don't think I can do that."

"Relax—you're not going to be practicing up here. Octavia has set up some ropes to practice on in the dance studio. I just wanted you to be able to visualise what the end goal in mind is here."

"Talk about a baptism of fire," I mumble, feeling muzzy headed as fear tears through me like a struck match.

"No, we're not having any of that," Midnight states sternly. He completely throws me with his comment. Before I know what's happening, he grabs me from around the waist and jumps off the stage while holding me, aiming towards the rope again. I scream so loudly as we become momentarily airborne, and I'm sure I must have shattered glass somewhere.

My eyes are squeezed shut tight until I manage to relax just enough to open them. However, before my equilibrium can rebalance itself, Midnight flips us upside down to where I do truly feel as if I'm about to lose breakfast.

Once the stage has been lowered again and we are back on terra firma, I am as white as a sheet.

"There's our star of the—oh my God, Darla, what is the matter?" Eva exclaims as she approaches us backstage.

"I think Midnight has broken her," I hear Medley state sarcastically, walking away and muttering that he's off to meet the others in the dance studio for rehearsals.

"She will be fine. Everyone's a bit shaky doing this the first time. I will continue her 'desensitisation' work this week until she's flying herself," Midnight declares confidently. I don't feel anywhere near confident with my legs still feeling like jelly.

"Are you sure you're okay, Darla? It's not too much too fast, is it? Bella was known for her great acrobatic skills up there, but she was used to it. If you don't feel ready, then –"

"No, I can do it. I *want* to do it. Besides, what is the point in having

195

this fantastic, once in a lifetime opportunity if I don't fully grasp it with both hands? I'm ok—I'm ready."

"Ok, well only if you are one hundred percent sure. Promise me if something becomes too much or too far out of your comfort zone that you'll let myself or someone else know," Eva says, watching me with a worried expression.

Funny how she can show concern over this being far out of my comfort zone but not my birthday. Guess I don't even get to pick and choose my fears these days either then! I think bitterly but then remind myself this *is* Pink Club and to stop thinking like a stroppy teenager.

"I promise. Honestly, if I didn't believe I could do this, I'd say something," I assure her as I internally wince, thinking how easily the white lie just trips off my tongue with bile still swirling inside my stomach.

"Good. Ok, well in that case, she's all yours, Midnight." Eva is smiling while trotting away in her pale pink kitten heels, her pink ponytail bouncing proudly behind her.

"Come on. Octavia and the guys are waiting. We are eating into rehearsal time, and it will take you a good while before you're competent enough to use the silk ropes by yourself," Midnight tells me, leading the way back to the dance studio.

As we enter the studio, the soundtrack 'Gold Digger' is blasting out of the speakers and the guys look well and truly warmed up.

"There she is! Our woman of the hour!" Octavia exclaims while dancing her way over to pull me forward.

We stand in staggered lines as Octavia begins the set again. It takes me a few moments, but I soon find my rhythm and am encouraged to take things freestyle. We go in turns to take the floor as we stand in a small circle, cheering each other on.

When the track finishes, we take a moment to catch our breath before I notice Octavia and Midnight prepping the space with silk ropes, which they thread through gold brass hoops affixed to the ceiling.

"Ok, gentleman—thank you for such a great warm up set today. I must now kindly ask you if you wouldn't mind going away to train backstage as Midnight and I get Darla acquainted with her new friends, the silk ropes," Octavia calls out while beaming one of her wonderfully bright supermodel smiles.

A small crash mat is put underneath the ropes.

"Ok, so today we're going to make this really fun and are going to gently break you in by teaching you how to do some spins, straddles and splits."

"I don't think what Midnight just did could be classed as 'breaking me in gently.'" I toss him under the bus, still feeling mad at what he did to me up on the high stage.

"What did you do?" Octavia demands, turning on Midnight.

"I just took our girl here for a little flying lesson," he grins wickedly.

"Ok, that's it—come on out. Today is going to be just us girls. You don't have the patience for teaching anyway."

Midnight looks as if he's about to say something but stays quiet, and the look is quickly replaced with a look of recognition as he just nods in agreement before walking out.

"Right! Let's begin, shall we?" Octavia approaches the silks. "First, you're going to wrap your right leg around, and you're just going to put your left foot on there…then push through and climb up—like this," Octavia instructs. She is making the move she just demonstrated look effortless and easy.

"The trickiest part to the climb is when your knees come up, and you position yourself like so. Then from here, you're going to stand up," Octavia continues.

"Looks…simple enough," I shrug, waiting for Octavia to descend so that I can then attempt this myself.

"Yes…now straighten that right leg. Good…two hands up— you're going to do a knee up, grab and push. *Yes,* Darla! Amazing! You got it; great job." Octavia's encouragement gives me the confidence I need to go on. By the end of the lesson, I've learned how to do quite a few positions and stretchy poses. I know in the morning I'm certainly going to feel muscles I never knew I had.

"You did so well today. Your abdominal strength and flexibility certainly help you a lot here."

"Pole dancing seems to be paying off –"

"Wait…you know how to *pole dance?!*"

"Yeah, it's where I…worked…before I came here…" I realise I've said too much about my sordid dance history and fear the worst now, as I'm expecting Octavia to expel me from the studio before telling all to Eva and having me frog marched off the property.

"Wow…I *love* the pole! We should book in some practice hours for sure. I'll be in touch to arrange some. Right, well, I'd better get my butt into gear; I've got a date with a celeb couple who are soon to be wed. They are having their after-party here."

"Wait, what? People get…*married* here as well?"

"Not married, *per se*, but they do have their wedding parties here, and Pink Club offers lessons for couple's first dances from *Moi*."

"That is so cool. So, whose getting hitched?"

"Now Miss Pebble, there are even some things Pink Club staff can't tell other Pink Club staff," Octavia says, winking at me. "Oh, and before I leave: if you ever want to do some pole practice, this button right here will bring the pole into the room. Press it again once you're done to retract it." Octavia presses the button on the wall, and it does indeed bring a pole into the room via a small, concealed compartment on the floor. It connects to what must be a magnet or something in the ceiling before there's a clicking noise, which must mean it's fixed into place.

"Thanks. I'll pretend I'm not the least bit jealous or interested to know who this celebrity couple are that you're about to rub shoulders with."

"You should be! The guy looks like the actor from 'Thor'."

"Oh-my-god…*pleasssee* let me come with you."

"Sorry, no can do," Octavia says teasingly before walking out of the studio. She swishes her hips from side to side and blows me a kiss through the glass doors.

We wave each other off and soon it is just me and my tool of mastery in the room: the pole.

* * * * *

"How did our girl get on?" Eva asks as Octavia enters her office.

"She's a natural, and you'll never guess what else."

"Oh, do tell."

"Darla is a professional pole dancer."

Eva splutters as she chokes on her sip of pink lemonade. "Yes, I knew she worked at...yes, I knew."

"Hey, it's great for fitness and it was probably a good job. Don't be so judgmental," Octavia lectures scornfully.

"Oh, yeah, sorry. I forgot you teach pole dancing."

"Exactly...and I am no stripper."

"Sorry V. Anyway, so she's doing good then...on the silk ropes?"

"Like I said, our girl is a natural. Do you know if my clients are here yet for their lesson?"

"Yes, I welcomed them in about an hour ago. You'll find them in the Pelican Brief Bar."

"Right, better get my butt into gear then."

"Before you go, where's Darla?"

"I left her rehearsing in the dance studio. She's practicing her pole dancing. I haven't seen her use the pole yet, but I have a feeling if you go and watch her, you won't be disappointed."

"You know something, I think I may just do that."

~ *Chapter 35* ~

It feels so good to be back in my element again with the pole. My body sings as my muscle memory kicks into gear. I can feel where I've lost a bit of conditioning and the areas that will need working on. After the silk ropes and this today, I'm going to be aching a lot tomorrow, but the sense of familiarity does feel good.

"That was bloody brilliant!"

"Ahh!" I yelp, realising too late that Eva is standing just inside the doors to the studio.

"Sorry to startle you," she chuckles.

"That's ok…I'm a little bit embarrassed, actually."

"Why on earth would you be embarrassed? Those are some magnificent feats of strength and skill you have there, Darla."

My cheeks flush pink from Eva's compliments. "So, it's ok that I was a pole dancer in a strip club?"

"When Octavia mentioned about your *old* job, I admit I immediately judged you until Octavia reminded me that she actually teaches just such a skill. And you had mentioned that early on, so you were honest. Nothing gives me the right to be so high and mighty, so

I hope you can…forgive me? Anyway," she continues before I answer. "We all have to sit on the toilet after all, even the queen. So what Joshua and Stella don't know…they don't know, okay?"

"Thanks," is all I can say, looking adoringly at the pole and caressing it with my hand like a trusty old friend.

"Good! Now that is the air cleared between us, do you fancy a spot of lunch?"

"I'm so hungry I could eat a horse," I admit.

Just then, Eva's mobile rings and the look on her face tells me lunch will have to wait. "So sorry to have to do this but…rain check?"

"Certainly. No worries. I'll finish up here and then should I meet you back at your office?"

"Yes, and if I'm not there I'll let Max know you're on your way so at least one of us will be there."

"Ok, cool. See you in a bit then."

"See you shortly." Eva dashes off like a mini pink tornado.

I then realise I don't have the map to help me get about. Thankfully, I do have my key card on me so at least I can get in and out of rooms. "Come on, feet," I tell myself as I head out of the dance studio. I follow the carpet towards the corridor where Joshua Glass's office is, stopping a moment when I hear a man yelling at someone.

Holy shit! Is he in the building? I can feel my heart starting to pound, as whoever he is shouting at is really getting it in the neck. The door is ajar, and against my better judgment, I peek in and see Joshua Glass shouting. He isn't shouting at a person, but rather down the phone line.

"I'm fed up with these stupid games of yours, Stella. You can't keep threatening me with my money. I know damn well what's at stake here. Go back to your husband—or do I need to inform him of exactly what has been going on here? Now, unless you have something business related to talk to me about, then just leave me the fuck alone!"

Shit! I should NOT be hearing this, I think just as I'm about to bolt.

"Just a minute, Miss Pebble," I hear him say which stops me dead in my tracks. I think I'm about to pass out. "Come in here, please. I know you're out there; I can see you on the camera."

I look up and notice there is, indeed, a small CCTV camera pointing directly at me. Giving a feeble wave, I turn back to enter Joshua Glass's office.

"Please, have a seat. I'm sorry you had to hear that phone call." He almost looks as if he is going to smile, but it vanishes before it can even happen.

Standing and walking over to me, gently he guides me with one of his big manly hands, pressing ever so slightly against the small of my back towards a black chair with bright plush pink upholstery that sits the opposite side of his desk. The sensation of his hand against my lower back sends a flurry of happy hormones that spike throughout my body, turning my cheeks red.

It is from my seated position that I begin to take in the scenery around me. This office is a far cry from the warmth that Eva's gives off with her coffee and cream tones. Joshua's room is harshly decorated in black and white with elements of steel undertones. An enormous black and white mounted photograph of Mimi laughing sits directly behind Joshua's desk, and for some reason this causes me an emotional pang in my heart, knowing this was his twin sister—literally the other half of him.

"It's a good thing I heard you call me into your office. I'd have hated to have appeared rude by walking on by, as I had my headphones in," I say, pointing towards my small earbud headphones dangling round my neck.

Good quick thinking, Miss Pebble! I think, congratulating myself.

"Yes, it is a good thing. Well done again on winning the position here at Pink Club. It was very well earned. I hope all our staff have been making you feel welcome."

"Everyone has been very kind and making me feel right at home here," I say, feeling my cheeks redden being alone with Joshua Glass…in his office, better able to see and smell him.

Dear God, woman—you're not the wolf out of Little Red Riding Hood!

"Good, because after Midnight's little stunt earlier, I'm now wondering how best to discipline him. Being so reckless like that endangering both your lives –"

"I'm sorry…that was my fault." *Woman, are you suicidal?!* my conscience thinks as the words just seemed to fall out before I could stop them.

"Your fault? Do tell," Joshua says. He leans back in his black leather office chair while resting his elbows up onto the arm rests, clasping both hands together. He gives me a look that makes me feel as if he sees straight through me.

"I…asked him to…show me some of his impressive rope moves."

"And how, pray-tell, does that make what he did *your* fault?"

"Because I said…"

"Yes?"

"I said…" *Shit—what could I have said?*

Just then Joshua's phone rings. *Phew! Saved by the bell!*

"Sorry, I have to take this, but it was great to see you again, Darla. Are you ok to see your own way out?"

"Yes, thank you. Bye," I mumble, rapidly exiting Joshua Glass's office. My heart is pounding away as the adrenaline that has been coursing throughout my body begins to ever so slightly calm down.

Just like that, my briefest conversation with my new boss was over. Eva had said he is more like a ghost around Pink Club since Mimi's death, so I relax in the thoughts that it will probably be a long time again until I see him; long enough for him to forget about Midnight's indiscretion.

Once I have made it down to the main reception area, Max spots me and asks if I would like a ride home. I graciously accept his offer, so he makes the necessary arrangements to have another one of his security guys drop me back as he has to stay around in case Joshua needs him.

Once back in the peace and quiet of my new surroundings, I decide to run myself a bath. Binks is sleeping soundly on the white fluffy rug that sits in front of the fireplace.

Sinking into the relaxing warmth of the water, I take a moment to reflect on all the craziness that is my life right now—the water helping to melt any tension and stress away. All of a sudden, an overwhelming and crushing sense of fear overtakes my body and I sit up in the water, grasping my knees to my chest, breathing rapidly and shivering as fear hits me again and again in waves. At one point, I feel as I'm about to die. Clambering out of the bath, I grab a towel and sit on the heated stone floor of the bathroom until the moment has passed. "What the fuck just happened?!"

Binks, sensing something was wrong, comes into the bathroom, meowing at me as if he's making sure—in cat language—that I am ok.

"Hi, buddy. I'm ok. I'm ok," I say more to myself then to him. His presence makes me feel more relaxed. Once my breathing is back to normal, I climb back into the bath where, this time, I manage to relax uninterrupted until the water is almost cold.

Still feeling unnerved by what happened in the bathroom, I decide to take my mind off things by watching a nice Christmas romcom on TV before getting a good night's sleep. Hopefully, whatever happened was just a one-off thing and I wouldn't need to worry about going through something like it again, as it was really scary.

~ *Chapter 36* ~

Heading into work, I see that there is much more activity going on than usual.

"Good morning, Darla," Eva greets cheerily while carrying a huge vase of Christmas flowers.

"Hi…er, can I help you with that?" I ask, finding it uncomfortable to see her struggling.

"Yeah, sure, here." She hands me the vase of flowers, which I hazard a guess must weigh at least twelve kg's. She then guides me off towards the main ballroom area and helps me place the vase atop a small white pillar. "It is the bride and groom's wedding today, so it's all hands-on deck," Eva says, puffing.

"Woah! The place looks completely transformed. What's with the staging area?" I ask, seeing a fine mist rolling off the surface of the ground stage.

"It's been turned into an ice rink; they have professional skaters coming in for a private performance of 'Snow White on Ice.'"

"Sounds dreamy." I take in the surroundings. The entire space has been turned into an enchanted Christmas themed forest. "What I wouldn't give to meet and marry my Prince Charming," I manage to mutter, trying to picture what that might look like.

"You and me both. Right, come on. Octavia is waiting in the dance studio, and I've got a tsunami of emails to respond to after I put the word out about our New Year's Eve bash, featuring a premier of our newest dancing star."

"I'm sorry, did you just say—you went ahead and planned for me to dance on New Year's Eve? Sorry, I thought it had only been merely an idea."

"Think of it more like a rehearsal to get you used to the crowd and that sort of thing," Eva says nonchalantly like it's no big deal.

"But I told you—that's my *birthday*."

"Correct. That is a problem because…?"

"Well…my mum and I—we normally celebrate it together."

"Darla, look around you. This is your life now. I'm sorry if you *used* to do things a certain way before working here, but we have all had to make sacrifices to be here. Can't you do something on a different day with your mum?"

"I really don't have a say on this, do I?"

"Afraid not…sorry," Eva said, giving a fake sympathetic look in my direction.

The puppet feeling returns, making me feel uneasy. I think how this is perhaps what drove Bella to taking drugs. There always seems to be a theme to fortune and fame with drug and alcohol abuse if stars like Amy Winehouse or Bella have taught us anything.

Was this a mistake after all? I think worriedly but quickly scrub it from my mind.

"Yes, you're right. I'm being a wimp. Sorry."

"Don't sweat it. Now, run along. Octavia is already warming up with the guys. Oh, and here—you'll need this. I'll catch up with you later," Eva remarks. She places a red and white striped elf hat, complete with a bell on the end, upon my head before promptly disappearing.

Heading off to the dance studio, jingling all the way, the overwhelming sense of panic hits me again and I find myself needing to dive into the nearest restroom. Wave after wave of this crushing feeling of fear hits me again and again. My breathing is erratic, and I feel like I'm about to have a heart attack.

Of all the people to call, I think I surprise even myself by dialling in my mum's number, and after a few rings she answers. "Darla! Darla? Are you ok? What on earth is the matter?" my mum exclaims on hearing me gasping for breath.

"I…f-feel…like…I can't…b-breathe!" I manage to stammer out through the mouthpiece of my mobile.

"Ok, don't worry, it sounds very much like a panic attack. Now, here is what I want you to do." My mum explains an exercise called the Havening whereby I have to close my eyes and imagine her and I walking along a beach while stroking the sides of my arms. I count to twenty and she then instructs me to open my eyes and look right and then left a few times. Amazingly, the technique works, and before I know it, I have full control over my body and breathing again.

"That's it. Just breathe. You got this," Mum says soothingly.

"Thanks, Mum. How did you know how to do that?"

"Therapy does have its charms at times. I decided to go back to my therapist. You are so right, darling—I *do* need to sort my life out.

I've made some terrible choices and treated you appallingly. I hope one day you can forgive me." I hear Mum's voice crack on the end of the phone and my heart breaks for her, but I do my best to remain strong.

"I'm really happy to hear you are back in therapy again and that it's working. Thank you for helping me realise what was happening to me and for the exercise. Listen, I have to run, but…do you want to meet for coffee tomorrow?"

"I'd really love that," Mum responds, suddenly sounding much happier.

"Great! Consider it a date. I'll meet you at Angel Cake at, say, 12:30?"

"It's actually my day off, so that's perfect."

"Ok, I'll see you then. Oh, and Mum? I love you."

"Love you too, sweetheart."

I click off the call and realise how late I am for rehearsals. I rapidly make my way up to the dance studio.

"We were beginning to wonder what on earth had happened to you," Octavia remarks as I take my place in front of the guys. Their faces show disdain at my tardiness.

Everyone's dressed in funny Christmas outfits.

"Sorry, I got a bit lost. Still getting my bearings here."

"No worries. As Eva has moved your first performance to New Year's Eve, we are going to need to do a lot of grafting for this. How are you for Christmas? Do you have any family plans we need to work around?"

"No…we don't really do the Christmas thing. My mum and I…well, it's usually take-away and rom-com movies." I realise how sad and pathetic that must sound. It was only magical at Christmas when I saw my grandparents, but as they were both dead now, the point of celebrating seemed lost for me.

"Oh…right. Well, how do you feel about having your first dance performance bumped up?" Octavia asks, a look of concern etched on her face.

"Actually, I'm not as anxious as I thought I would be." And it's true; I feel eerily calm considering this huge bombshell has just been dropped on me. Maybe I am getting used to everything so much so now that my fear is not so magnified anymore.

Siren approaches me from the back of the studio dressed as Olaf the snowman. "Darla –"

"Nice costume," I joke.

"Why, thank you. Now, listen…as a retired police officer, and having extensive knowledge of health and safety with stage rigging and lighting, I have proposed that we fit you with a safety harness for the performance."

"Won't that break the illusion, though? You know, with a great big harness over my body?"

"Special effects can get around that. Joshua also wants to ensure you are safe up there," Octavia joins in, reassuring me. She's wearing an elf dress with fishnet tights and elf-styled boots with bells on.

"I'm happy to wear the harness, but I'm also happy not to wear it. Whatever you decide, though, I will gladly go along with."

"Don't be stupid, Darla. It's very dangerous up there. What if you slip or fall?" Mixer chimes in, which starts an eruption of heated debate between all of them. It's quite hilarious watching elves, reindeer and a snowman all bickering.

"HEY!" I yell then whistle to grab everyone's attention. "Look— I said I'm happy either way. I trust you guys to do your job properly to keep me safe up there, so just let me know when everything is one hundred percent decided and I'll go along with it...ok?"

A brief silence creeps along the air before Octavia pipes up. "You really think you can do the performance without the harness?"

"Yes—I *really* do."

"Ok, then I'm happy to give you the chance. Now, this idea doesn't leave this room...do I make myself clear? There's *no way* Joshua will clear this, and if Darla is to have a real chance at experiencing just what it's like up there, I think she's more then up to the task," Octavia tells everyone. She swears all of us to an unwritten code of silence.

"It's your funeral, but okay; I'll go along with it," Digit grumbles, which gets the rest of the guys to mumble their agreement to keep quiet.

"Right! No time like the present. We'd better start rehearsing on the stage today." Mixer leads the way out of the studio.

"Are you an adrenaline junkie or something? Because you sure have bigger kahunas than I do," Octavia chuckles as we step outside.

"Hey, isn't there a wedding on today? How can we rehearse?" I remember how beautifully decorated the ballroom had been.

"We are going to a less...conventional practicing area for today's lesson," Octavia replies cryptically.

Her response puts me slightly on edge. "Where might that be?" I inquire, as the familiar sense of unease begins to uncoil like a snake in my stomach before travelling up my spine.

"No point freaking you out until we actually get there," is all she says, which does nothing to alleviate my nerves.

Leaving en-masse, I realise we are going a different way to get outside of Pink Club. We walk through numerous winding corridors backstage where I can hear violins playing sweet melodic wedding music. I'm tempted to grab a sneak peek at the bride and groom but don't get a chance because I'm gently nudged forward by Medley, who is walking directly behind me.

Once we are outside, we split into two groups. The guys all clamber inside a big four-by-four truck driven by Midnight, and Octavia and I hop onto her green and black Yamaha motorbike.

"I've never been on a motorbike before," I admit as adrenaline begins coursing through my body with a sense of anticipation and excitement.

"You had better hold on tight then," she instructs as we take off our elf hats and replace them with protective helmets. She kicks the bike into gear before we speed away. The sudden acceleration makes my stomach momentarily churn and I grip Octavia around the waist for grim death.

"Hey, try to relax." Her voice comes through a small speaker inside my helmet, which is when I realise they must have hidden microphones connected via Bluetooth.

"This is so cool!" I exclaim as fear gives way to exhilaration.

Octavia ducks and dives through streets and narrow roads. My heart momentarily leaps into my mouth as a pedestrian goes to cross the street right in front of us, but upon seeing the bike, he makes the sensible decision to take a big step back and away from the crossing as we zoom past.

Eventually, we come to a stop in what looks like a car park in front of a derelict building. The guys arrive shortly afterwards in Midnight's truck.

"Welcome to our urban training ground," Octavia announces, flashing me one of her perfect white super models smiles. As she leads the way inside, I see that this is definitely a warehouse of sorts. In the middle is a big container that has been suspended on cables.

"Wow—this place is HUGE!" I exclaim, turning around as we venture further inside so that I can take it all in.

"Ok, bring it down," Midnight instructs as Digit does what is asked of him.

"Wait a minute…am I going to dance on –"

"The floating container? Yep. It's not the size of the stage at Pink Club but should help you get spaciously aware for when we perform on New Year's Eve."

"I take it there is no crash mat here then?"

"Nope; but don't worry—we'll get you dancing on it while it's on the ground first and gradually rise you up. Don't overthink it," is all Midnight says before going to help the guys. They attach the silk ropes they brought with them through huge industrial strength hooks. Music begins to play from somewhere out across the vast open space and I recognise it's Coldplay's "A Head Full of Dreams."

"Time to get on board," Medley says, winking at me before guiding me to a concrete block on the floor where he tells me to climb onto his shoulders.

I'm shivering from the cold air outside but I'm assured that we will all soon be toasty warm as tall standing outdoor heaters have been switched on and are pointing at the makeshift elevated stage.

The sensation when he stands up to full height once I am perched upon his broad shoulders makes me screech for a split second before I feel balanced. He then walks over towards the metal container that is now on the ground. Midnight, Digit, Mixer and Siren are already on the top with Octavia directing from the ground.

Medley and I approach and Mixer gives me one of his hands, helping to pull me up. The top of the container has been altered to become a smooth surface perfect for dancing upon. Four silk ropes hang just on the outside of the container at each corner.

"Ok, listen up. You won't be able to do the whole routine up there, but we can hone your skills on getting you used to leaping and catching the silk ropes before swinging back," Octavia tells me, starting my lesson.

"Not before she puts this safety harness on, she isn't," Medley growls, which elicits eye rolls and sighs from the rest of the group. He is already slipping the harness over my head and clipping it around my waist. He adjusts the straps until its secure, then attaches the harness to a hook on a rope of bungee cord material.

"I rigged up some specialist staging wires they use for shows where characters or dancers need to fly around or across the stage," he explains.

"If you're quite ready, let's begin," Octavia commands like a pro.

"Woah! Woah! Woah! What are you doing?!" I yell, alarmed as Mixer grabs a rope attached to my harness and pulls which makes me travel up and backwards. I'm now raised up to where just the tips of my trainers scrape the top of the container.

"I am getting you to fly, of course," he responds. He lets go of the rope and the momentum sends me flying forward.

"Ahhhhhhhh!" I scream as vertigo hits me like a punch in the guts.

"Open your arms," Midnight calls, but my hands won't let go of the harness.

I fly back towards the container where Mixer grabs my harness belt, but instead of helping to stop me, he this time starts running clockwise with me before letting go.

"You can do it, Darla! Let go, let go…NOW!" Octavia yells from the ground.

On trusting her, I gingerly let go, and as I do, I gracefully begin to float around and around while suspended by the bungee cord I'm affixed to. As I slowly open my arms, I am instructed to lift my knees up and out while bringing my feet together. This position gives me better control, and once I'm balanced and swing closer to the platform, Mixer catches me, helping to bring me to a slow stop.

"That was such a crazy rush. Can I go again?"

Everyone cheers and claps with a few air punches.

"You got your wings, girl. Welcome—*officially*—to the gang!" Siren cheers, affixing a small pink pin of wings just under the collar of my T-shirt.

"Right—time to get busy," Octavia snaps as the music is turned up.

I am lowered to the point where my feet touch the base of the modified container unit. All Octavia wants me to get used to first is running and jumping off the platform and grabbing a hold of a silk rope before wrapping it around my foot, balancing myself before swinging back to the platform. She does ask if I want to attempt it without the harness, but I admit my confidence is not quite there yet.

We proceed to practice the rest of my dance routine on solid ground, as we can't all safely fit on top of the container. On the ground further off to the right is a painted outline of the exact stage parameters back at Pink Club, which does, indeed, resemble that of a Celtic cross.

"Who came up with the design for the stage?" I ask Octavia as we set up on the faux stage.

"Mimi and Joshua's great-grandmother wore a golden Celtic cross necklace, which had been gifted to her by their grandfather when they were married after World War II. They both went over Stella's head to get the stage built and organised as it had already been in the twins' original plans before Stella came and took everything away from them."

"That is such a beautiful sentiment. What I don't understand, though, is if Stella has so much money, why is she only *renting* the establishment? How come she didn't buy it outright?"

"Because she likes to control things. She's someone who wants all the recognition but does little to no work to make it all happen."

"Why didn't they both just walk away?" I'm still confused at the hold this 'Stella' has on Pink Club.

"Sorry, not really my place to answer that question. Try asking Eva. She knows more about the guts of the issues than me. What I can tell you is whatever Stella has on Joshua must be serious, as it really did make him heel to her. Right. Come on, enough gasbagging. Time to refine your skills. The clock is ticking, after all."

Octavia's mention of time brings my sense of bubbling trepidation to full throttle throughout my heart and body as I further embrace my new role of lead dancer for Pink Club.

~ *Chapter 37* ~

"Hi, Mum. Sorry I'm late. Work has been manic," I greet, plonking myself down into a chair opposite Mum inside of Angel Cake. Christmas music fills the space and the decorations are already up, making the place feel really festive.

"Don't worry about it. I've been so worried about you since your panic attack yesterday."

My mother…worried about me? "Honestly I am fine. Your magic did the trick."

"Just as long as you're ok—that's all that matters," my mum responds. I can tell by her eyes that she's really genuine this time.

"Hello, ladies. What can I get for you today?" Katia greets us brightly, standing a with pen in hand poised over her notebook, ready to take our order.

"We will have two afternoon teas with finger sandwiches and scones, please," I order.

"I insist you let me pay for this," my mother says sternly.

"Are you sure?"

"One hundred and ten percent sure. It's about time I started looking after you. Can you ever forgive me for being…doo-lally?"

"You're my mum and I love you—warts and all."

As we sit and chat, I can't get over the transformation in my mother. She's really thrown herself into her therapy this time and does everything she's been asked to do.

"Hang on, this therapist –"

"A very nice, handsome and utterly charming but happily married gay man."

Phew!

"You don't need to worry; I've taken a sabbatical from dating for at least the next year," Mum assures me with a grin.

"How have you been finding living on your own?"

"Do you know something? I find myself quite enjoying it, but I do have a little confession."

"Oh, God—what did you do?"

"I…got a puppy. He is a little French bulldog and is a rescue. His name is Diego," Mum confesses.

"Aw, have you got any pics?"

"Sure…here. Look, isn't he the cutest?"

I smile at the picture of Diego. "*Sooo* cute. I can't wait to come visit just so I can pet him."

Our food and drinks arrive, and I can't believe that my mum has really turned a corner in her life. I'm so proud of her.

Once our lunch date is over, I feel quite sad to know that I will be going back to my big empty apartment alone. Turning to Mum, feeling almost shy, I ask, "Mum…would you mind if I stayed over tonight?"

"Of course, darling! You can come over whenever you want. Is everything ok?"

"It's just been a really hectic few weeks and I miss you."

"I'll make up the spare bedroom then," Mum smiles happily.

"Yay! I just have to pop home to feed Binks and then I'll be right over."

Vera approaches with the card reader so Mum can settle the bill. She seems in much brighter spirits since her and Frank have employed Katia.

"Vera, might I have a quiet word with you?"

"Certainly. There you go," she says as she hands Mum the receipt.

"Right…well, I'll see you at home then," I tell Mum as she heads out of Angel Cake.

Vera turns to me with a quizzical look on her face. "What's on your mind, Darla?"

"I…have something to give you and Frank. Don't open it until I've gone," I tell her in a rushed voice so she won't argue.

"Why, thank you very much," Vera says as I pass her an envelope.

Earlier, I had written a cheque for one thousand pounds out of my account to give to Vera and Frank. I'm a big believer in acts of kindness and paying it forward, so I had also donated (anonymously online) quite a handsome sum of money to a charity fundraising page Dante had set up to help get a newer and much nicer community centre up and running.

As I turn to leave, Vera immediately opens the envelope and stops me in my tracks by grabbing my arm gently. "What on earth is this for?"

"You and Frank were very kind to me when I worked here. You

helped me in more ways than you'll know. Watching you both struggle…well, it just felt like a nice thing to do, and that money is for you to treat yourselves. Please say you'll accept it."

"I—don't know what to say. Thank you very much," Vera sniffs, graciously accepting my gift. She gives me a hug with tears in her eyes.

"The pleasure is all mine, really. Soon I may not be able to come in here quite so often as I'm going to be really busy with this new job of mine."

"You got a dancing job, didn't you—as in a *proper* dancing job?"

I never could keep anything from Vera. She had become almost like a mum figure to me, helping me cope better when things were not so good at home by counselling me.

"Yes, but I'm not supposed to tell anyone about it. Please don't mention it to anyone else."

"Now that is some very good news to hear, indeed, and don't you worry—Mum's the word," Vera promises, making an invisible zipping motion across her lips.

Frank approaches me just before I'm about to step out of the door, and I watch Vera carefully slide the envelope inside her apron pocket while winking at me outside of sight of her husband.

"See you soon, Darla," Franks nods while holding the door open for me.

"Wait! Here is our email address," Vera calls after me. She quickly scribbles her email address on her notepad before handing me the piece of paper.

"Oh—are you going somewhere then?"

"Darla is going on an adventure. Now come on—stop being so

nosey. We've got customers to serve," Vera chastises, steering Frank away from me and the door, looking back just briefly to wink at me.

Another chapter from my old life now closed. The truth is, if—or when—it ever gets known that I dance for Pink Club, I highly doubt I will just be able to frequent old haunts such as Angel Cake with the freedom I previously had. The thought saddens me but also reflects to me just how much my life has changed. A sense of pride fills my heart as I walk away.

Staying the night at Mum's was just what I needed to get a good night's sleep and recharge my batteries. An odd thought, as living with her used to be the root cause as to just *why* my batteries used to feel drained, but it has been good spending quality time with her and her new four-legged companion, Diego, who is really adorable.

Out of habit, I check the and freezer and am taken aback to see that she has been cooking her own meals from FRESH ingredients and freezing the leftovers! There is also plenty of food in the fridge as well, and I notice she has placed a floral calendar on the wall where days of the weeks have been organised with cookery classes, therapy sessions, puppy school for Diego and aqua aerobics. A wave of emotion hits me, and I realise just how proud of her I am. It seems like me moving out really was the right decision after all. The relief in knowing this was the right move for us as mother and daughter washes over me and a weight feels like it has been lifted off my shoulders.

* * * * *

The next day, I deliberately vacate early for dance rehearsals but leave a note for Mum on the fridge with some money for her to treat herself to anything she wants. I'm happy to find out Trevor is on shift when I call the number. I need him to take me home so I can freshen up before heading off to Pink Club for rehearsals.

"Mornin', Darla. Is it back home you would like me to drop you?"

"Good morning, Trevor. Yes, please drop me off home."

He doesn't mention the last time he dropped me at my mother's where she was running around like some half-crazed lunatic, and I don't offer any explanation. The drive home is quite pleasant; the roads are quiet, save for the early risers like me who can be seen making their necessary journeys via car or bicycle.

On entering my apartment, Binks comes rushing over to me and I give my little furry friend his obligatory cuddle. Once he has been fed and watered, I call Max to arrange a pickup to Pink Club.

"Good morning, Darla. How may I help you?" Max answers.

"May I please have a lift into work?"

"Certainly. Would you like me to come now?"

"If you could pick me up in the next hour that would be great."

Max must have momentarily placed his hand over the mic because he doesn't answer right away, but I can hear unintelligible voices in the background. "Hi—sorry, Darla. Yes, I can pick you up within the hour."

I thank him before hanging up. My tummy rumbles, alerting me to the fact I haven't had any breakfast, so have decided to make myself some mini vanilla pancakes. Just as I place the last morsel of pancake in my mouth, my doorbell rings. When I check, I see Max waiting. I let him inside and quickly change my clothes for dance rehearsal, then follow Max down to the underground carpark.

A sudden bright flash discombobulates me as we head towards the car, and within what must have been a split second, and as my vision begins to clear, I see Max on the ground, wrestling with a man who is dressed from head to toe in black. Max tears a camera out of his hands and pulls out what looks to be a SIM card and pockets it. The man scrambles to his feet, both breathless (Max less so). Max lets him go but throws the camera to the ground.

"Now fuck off, you piece of scum," Max growls threateningly.

The man says nothing but instead pulls out a smaller handheld camera out of his black hoodie pocket and lifts it up. This pushes Max over the edge and he sprints towards the individual. The two men disappear out of sight as Max chases after him. He returns a short while later with the man's other camera in his hand, which looks as if it is splattered with blood.

"Are you ok?" he asks me, placing a reassuring hand on my shoulder as I am helped into the car.

"I'm fine. What happened to the photographer?"

"I doubt he will be coming here again to cause trouble. Don't get out of the car. I will be back momentarily," Max orders.

Doing as I'm told, I wait anxiously for Max to reappear.

"Right, now that's sorted, and we can finally get you into work. I will need to inform Joshua that the paps have been sniffing around Bella's old apartment. There must be a leak somewhere. Until we know what's going on, you will have to be relocated, I'm afraid."

"Oh…and I was just getting to feel a home in my new apartment."

"Side effect of the job, I'm afraid." I sense Max is still stressed from the earlier fight and take the hint to keep small talk to a minimum.

He raises a small glass partition so that I can't hear the conversation he's now having with someone and probably has to do with what just happened.

On arrival to Pink Club, Max helps me out of the car and informs me that an emergency meeting has now been called, so he must leave me to make my own way inside the building. I can't shake the feeling that the man in the carpark is somehow my fault, but I honestly haven't told anyone about where I am now working. Dante and Sarah are the only two people who know about it, and they had to sign heavy agreements, which meant that if they did divulge any information, it would be legally very bad for them.

I also can't shake the sinister feeling that these occurrences will soon become the norm for my life as I hand over my simple, uncomplicated life for one of glitz and glamour. My life would now become a label a brand which was stated in my contract.

Well, nothing to be done about it now; it's everything I ever wanted, so I'll just have to put my big girl pants on, pull my socks up, and stride ahead, putting my best dancing foot forward.

I walk into the corridors of Pink Club with my mind drifting from one thought to the next of an uncertain future, and—to my horror— I realise I am lost.

Max has already taken my bag with meagre belongings inside, as no staff are allowed to have their mobile phones or personal possessions on them, so this means no phone, no map and zero sense of direction. Turning around, I decide to just follow the same wall back the way I had come in the hopes it would lead me to an area I recognised and could find my bearings from.

~ *Chapter 38* ~

Eva and Max are talking to Joshua via video link.

"I'm not sure how there has been a leak, but that man who was waiting for Darla in the carpark had clearly been tipped off," Max explains, his voice laced with concern.

"Speak to Darla and try to see if there is any way she may have inadvertently given away what her job is to someone," Joshua responds calmly, although beneath the surface—and unbeknown to Max and Eva—he is more than just a little upset at the recent complication.

"She does have two friends, Dante Collins and his girlfriend…Sarah? But they were there when Darla auditioned and signed the NDA's. Other than them, I don't know who else would know. Darla swears she has told no one else—not even her mother," Eva puts in, trying to take the heat off Darla and any suspicion that she had something to do with the leak.

"Ok…well, if you can't find a link from Darla, then we need to interview all staff here," Joshua states, and Eva suddenly feels unwell.

"That will take –"

"I don't care how long it takes, Eva…just do it. We need to keep the lid on this until New Year's Eve. Otherwise, Stella will have all our heads on a plate," Joshua interrupts before abruptly disconnecting the call.

"Charming. So…what should we do now?" Eva turns to Max who's looking very concerned as he stares at a screen showing live CCTV footage.

"I suggest you go and fetch out newest dancer before she becomes dog food."

Eva is momentarily puzzled until she looks at the screen herself. "Oh, shit!"

"Indeed," Max answers. He immediately gets on the radio to alert all of his security personnel that Darla is lost in the east basement wing of Pink Club and one of their Rottweiler security dogs has got out and is presently stalking her.

* * * * *

Where the hell am I? So much for my theory of following a corridor wall to take me back to where I started. I think my mistake was when I went through a door and followed stairs downward, thinking it would lead back to the underground carpark. Not only did I not think to count the number of flights I went down, but once I got to what must be a basement area of sorts, I somehow managed to get myself locked in down here.

It's terribly dark with low-level lighting and very cold. I've never felt so vulnerable without my mobile phone. I can see big electric boxes on one of the walls and decide to follow the only concrete corridor that seems to have more light shining down it. Following it to the end, and making a right, I'm happy to see concrete steps that lead up and outside. A set of fire escape doors are unlocked, and as I step outside, the fresh cool air feels so good on my face and body. It is also here I can see that this is like some sort of a courtyard area and there seems to be dog agility equipment dotted around.

How odd. Why on earth do they have dog training equipment here? Oh…of course…security dogs. Fear prickles along my skin as the hair on my body stands on end when the realisation hits me. Placating my fear, I tell myself that whatever security animals they have here will be kept in a secure location and they might not even keep the dogs on sight. *Calm down, Darla; everything will be fine. Someone will know you're missing soon and come to find you.*

The sky begins to spit with rain, and knowing it's not much warmer inside, I figure it's better to be dry and cold then wet and cold. I head back inside the dark basement area of the building. Unable to do anything until help arrives, I decide to begin running through some of the choreography I've been learning and am soon feeling warmer and more at ease as the dancing brings a much-needed distraction to my thoughts.

Suddenly, a loud bark breaks my reverie and I come to a startled stop. The barking is coming from the same door I entered through but then found I couldn't get back out of.

"Oh, thank God; they've found me." Approaching the door, I don't see anyone. I peer through the square pane of glass in the middle of the door and am startled by a huge black and tan Rottweiler who jumps up, barking, whining and licking at the door.

"Holy *shit!* Wait, calm down, Darla. The dog can't come in here;

the door is shut." My blood feels as if it has turned to ice in my veins, and to my horror, as I back away from the door, the huge dog uses its powerful jaws to clamp down onto the handle of the door the other side and proceeds to open it with ease. He whines and sniffs around me before playfully grabbing at my hands with his mouth.

My heart hammers away so fast and loudly that any—and all—thoughts seem to get drummed out by the loud *'thump' 'thump' 'thump'* of my pulse now hammering away inside my ears.

The dog eventually gives up the ghost of getting my attention and begins to trot towards the training area. Thinking quickly on my feet, I follow the enormous beast to the fire escape doors; he paws and pushes at them as if indicating he wants to go out, so I oblige him. Then, with my hand violently shaking, I press on the metal bar. Once the door opens, the beast bounds outwards, proceeding to gallop around the small space. Eventually, the dog comes back towards the door, and I sharply shut it, knowing this time he really can't regain entry.

My legs, like jelly, give way and I slump down on the top step. I can't tell if I'm shivering from being cold or because I've just had a close call with a huge brutish beast that could have torn me limb from limb.

Some time passes and I can hear the rain beginning to come down hard. The dog, having done its business, returns to the fire escape doors where he whines and paws at them as if pleading with me to let him in. As I stand and look at him through the glass, my heart softens, and his big black doggy eyes must have done something to my soul because the next thing I know, I'm opening the doors to let the monster back inside with me.

Ever so thankful to have been let back into where its dry, the dog shakes his wet fur all over me, covering me in wet dog water and slobber. *Eurgh! Gross! Some thanks for being a Good Samaritan.*

So…here we are: me and this new furry friend of mine sitting alone in semi-darkness, waiting for rescue.

"You don't seem so bad for a security dog. Ahh, now, let's see…you have a collar on. What does it say? Your name is Bane?" As I speak the beast's name, he barks loudly and suddenly stands upright and alert as if waiting further instruction. Having had pet dogs before, and going through the pleasurable experience of puppy schools, I try out some simple commands with Bane.

The door I came through slams shut, making us both jump. I watch as Bane growls and barks whilst cantering over to where he heard the sound.

"SIT!" A big booming male voice says, which bounces off the concrete walls.

"Hello, Miss…are you alright?" the man says with Bane now attached to a harness and leash.

"Yes, I'm quite alright—no harm done."

"Name's Oliver. I'm one of the dog training security team here at Pink Club. I take it you got yourself a bit lost, Miss…"

"Darla. Darla Pebble," I tell him as I shake his hand.

"This is Omega Fox. I have located and retrieved the missing person in question and dog. I'm bringing her to you now. Omega out." He speaks into a walkie-talkie device and I'm fascinated.

"Gosh, seeing how you all communicate is like watching a scene out of a Hollywood movie."

"Trust me, it really isn't like the movies would have you believe. Here, put this around you. You look frozen," Oliver says as he kindly places his huge suit jacket around my much smaller shoulders. The jacket is warm from his body heat which helps me to relax.

"You're pretty good…with the dog, I mean."

"Well, I don't have any experience with guard dogs, per se, but I have owned a few dogs in my time and attended some training schools for puppies. I just used what little I know about dog language to help Bane realise that I'm not a threat."

"You're lucky. Bane is one of the best alpha dogs we have. They aren't always on site here because they are trained and normally kept at another location by our security company. Max organises the hiring of staff and their dog handlers to big events around the U.K., not just here at Pink Club."

"I'm feeling a bit more thankful now for being both a cat *and* a dog person," I chuckle.

"You have cats? Me too! What breed?" Oliver brightens at the mere mention of my love of the felines.

"Just the one; he's a rescue, actually. He is a little British Blue called Binks."

"What a great name. Have you got any pics of him? This is my pride and joy, Leo. He is just the cutest ragdoll, don't you think?" Oliver pulls out a photo of his cat who is, indeed, really cute.

"Aww, he's really adorable. Sorry, I would show you mine, but…you know—not allowed phones on shift."

"Ah, perhaps another time then."

We walk all the way through the maze of corridors until we get to Eva's office. When I enter the office, Eva runs to me to make sure I'm ok.

"I'm so sorry about all of this. I lost my bearings, and the more I tried to find my way back the more lost I got," I assure her. I feel terrible for worrying everyone.

"Please don't apologise. Oliver, thank you. You may leave now with the beast."

Once Oliver is out of sight, Max approaches me with my mobile phone. "I thought we were not allowed our mobiles on us while at work," I comment, feeling puzzled.

"After today, we decided it would be wise for new employees to have the capacity to call in case of an emergency," Max tells me with a smile.

"You inadvertently showed a crack in the security protocol of what having no phone could mean, should someone get lost. Obviously, Max and his team do their best to train for every eventuality, but thanks to you, we've now tweaked the ruling on mobiles. So, for now, until you're confident enough to be without your phone, we think it wise if you always have it on you," Eva says brightly, though I sense an undertone to her voice.

Unbeknown to me, once the situation was clear as to what had happened to me once I'd gone missing and that there was a dangerous dog on the loose, tracking me, Eva and Max had been going toe to toe losing their shit, half expecting me to get eaten alive.

"Aren't you worried I'll take sneaky photos or videos and leak them to the press?"

"We trust you, but...can this be kept just between the three of us and these four walls for now?" Eva asks sheepishly.

"Okay...sure, my lips are sealed."

"Phew, good. Now, come on, you've got a busy day ahead of you. Octavia is already in the dance studio with the guys."

"What about the mystery man with the camera?"

"Our John Doe appears to have been staking out Bella's old apartment block for a while. When he noticed Eva coming and going, even in her incognito outfits...well, it wouldn't have taken a genius then to join the dots," Max states.

"So, my identity is –"

"Still an enigma, thankfully. He had not yet streamed anything to social media, and I was able to destroy any photographic evidence. I have some people who owed me a few favours, so let's just say I called them in. He won't be bothering you anymore or running his mouth to anyone."

Even though I have just been given a lot of reassurances by Max, I know more than most how not to trust people. That man could sell my identity to any tabloid newspaper and be paid handsomely for doing so.

"I see the cogs whirring in your mind, Darla. Is there anything else you'd like to ask me?" Max asks, reading my worried expression correctly.

"What's to say he won't sell my identity to the tabloids?"

"We have some...*sensitive* info on our John Doe that he would never wish to see the light of day. Don't worry—I have covered all bases."

"As far as reassurances go, I'll reserve judgment until we know for sure," I tell him as Eva promptly ushers me out of her office, pointing me in the direction of the Juliette staircase that will take me to the dance studio.

~ *Chapter 39* ~

"Ok, so from now on, we are to only be rehearsing in the main ballroom on the raised stage unless other functions are on," Octavia explains, which makes my stomach feel as if it's falling out of me. "You look worried…have you got something on your mind?" she asks pointedly. I swallow any concern as we head on towards the staging area.

"For the basis of training, I think Darla may benefit from having a safety harness until she's more confident; don't you agree?" Midnight interjects.

"I would really prefer if we did train with harnesses on…just for now," I agree, which elicits a grin from Midnight.

"*Good girl,*" he whispers into my ear.

It feels as if I have been struck with a match inside. My cheeks blush after his recognition that I can heel when need be and I'm not all about feisty-ness.

"Very well; I'll get costume to do a camouflaged harness just in case Darla is still a bit like Bambi up there on her first night," Octavia concedes, marching ahead.

"Hey, that's a cute nickname...Bambi," Siren chuckles.

I know forever now it will be my new pet-name for these guys but still better to have a friendly name than a bitchy name.

When I'm up on the stage, I realise that I am beginning to feel more and more at home there.

"Ok, turn...and turn....walk...walk....jump and spin...*aaaaaaand* down," Octavia instructs through a microphone that emits her voice through speakers so we can hear her up here.

I'm panting and sweat pours from all of us. The lights make it very hot, and there is a dizzying effect of the big screen which amplifies us so everyone inside will be able to see us dancing. This does take some getting used to.

"Ok, listen up! I know Darla feels more secure in the harness, but let's end today's session on a high note with the harness *off*. I want one good leap of faith to the silk rope where you will sit in swing posture before swinging back to the stage."

As Octavia gives her instruction, I feel queasy but remind myself that I've been doing this for weeks and can do this now. It's the same with or without the harness, and if I fall, there is a mechanism that will allow me a much softer landing than it did for Fixer the day Bella pushed him over the edge.

"Right...on my count: one...two...*three!*"

"Yahhhh!" I yelp as I leap like lady Tarzan off the stage, aiming towards the silk rope. I grab hold of the rope and get to work, focusing on getting into the swing seat pose and holding, until Octavia instructs me to go back to a simple loop around my foot, securing me. Then, as if I have been doing this my whole life, I effortlessly swing with control back to the stage. I have a bit of a stumble on the dismount, but otherwise it all goes smoothly.

"Well done, Darla; great work today. As long as you can do that on New Year's Eve, we'll all be sweet. Right, I'm off, guys. See you bright and early tomorrow for more rehearsals." Octavia does a little shimmy dance before waving as she walks out.

Midnight, Digit, Medley, Siren and Mixer give me a big applause and I can't help but become emotional. They come in close for a group hug before lifting me up and giving me the bumps. The exhilaration of the day will be hard to top.

We finally make it down to Terra Firma where the temporary darkness of the underground back staging area envelopes all of us.

"Hey, Bambi, we're going to go for a beer in The Pelican Brief before heading home. Fancy joining us in celebration of your milestone event?" Mixer asks with his well-chiseled facial features and come-to-bed eyes.

"Thanks for the offer, but maybe next time. I am beat."

"Ok, suit yourself…but next time is on you," Mixer says, winking at me while imitating firing off a gun with his hand.

I won't be needing any alcohol to feel all a dither ever again now that I have so much eye candy around me for what is nowadays a proportionately large amount of my time. This thought makes me realise just how much I miss human contact from the opposite sex.

Sighing, and feeling the loneliness of being single brings with it, I start to make my way out of Pink Club, pondering on what to have for supper and what movie to watch. My phone rings to life and on answering I can see it's Mum.

"Hi, Mum…is everything ok?" I ask tentatively. The last time I got a call from her it was to announce my grandmother's death.

"Yes. I just wondered if you were free tonight. I've got some news, and -"

"Sure, I'm free. What time shall I come over?"

"If you could make your way here promptly, I'd really appreciate it."

"Okay…are you sure everything is ok?"

"Yes, I'm fine; life is really good. So, see you in a bit then?"

"Cool, ok. Shall I bring pizza with me?"

"You read my mind. See you soon. Love you."

"Love you, too."

I collect my bag from the security locker when I'm accosted by Max and Eva.

"Darla, I'm glad we caught up with you before you left. Listen, you're not to use that taxi firm I recommended anymore. From now on, all your lifts must be organised through either Max or myself," Eva instructs while smiling. I sense it's a forced smile, and they look at each other momentarily as if something is going on.

"Right, well…if that's the case, is anyone free to drive me home now? My mum wants to see me as soon as possible, but I'll want to get showered and dressed at mine first." I shock myself at how annoyed my voice sounds, and how authoritarian the words came out of my mouth. I'm not usually so blunt, especially not with management from any job I've had. My concerns seem not to be valid, though, as Max happily arranges a driver named Eric to take me back home and then drive me to my mum's.

"Eric will meet you in the security office when you're ready to go," Max says, handing me my bag.

"Thank you. See you tomorrow," I call out as I head off in the direction of the office.

"Don't forget to call me or Max first before arranging travel," Eva says. I just raise a hand to wave while walking ahead to let her know I've heard her.

Eric is like a real-life superman in form. He is tall, broad-shouldered, and very, *very* handsome. If my man-candy list grows any longer, I'll be truly spoilt for choice of fantasy when I'm having some *'alone time'* to myself while in my bed or the bath.

"Miss Pebble, I presume. My name is Eric. It's a pleasure to meet you. Right, are you ready to go? Max said you wanted to leave sharpish."

"Y–yes…pleasure's all mine," I stammer. I know I've said my safety dance team are rather *yummy*, but here is a man I'd happily have a dalliance with—perhaps a *few* dalliances.

Eric gets me safely home where I do a rapid shower and change of clothes before heading off to Mum's.

"Oh, bugger!" I cry as I climb into the car.

"Have you forgotten something, Darla?"

"I told my mum I'd grab pizza on the way."

"Not a problem," Eric says, lifting his phone to his ear. "Hello, Papa José's? Yes, I'd like to make an order for…"

"Two medium pepperoni, thin crust; two orders of garlic bread; and some chocolate cheesecake," I whisper to Eric as he makes the order. Eric reels off the order and Mum's address. The man is my hero…and my stomach rumbles as if to say it concurs.

Arriving safely at Mum's, I say a swift 'thank you' to gorgeous Eric, secretly hoping to have many more trips in the car with him, as he helps me exit the vehicle and walks me to the front door of Mum's apartment building. *Oh, be still my beating heart—what a chivalrous young man.*

"Hi, darling. How have you been? Let me take your coat." Mum smiles at Eric as he backs down the pathway towards the car.

"I'm good, thank you," I reply as Mum helps me out of my coat and hangs it on the rack by the door.

"No pizza?"

"It's on its way. My driver —" *Shit—my driver! What am I thinking? That's far too much information.*

"You mean the smart private taxi I just saw peel away from the kerb?"

"Yes…I —"

"Darla, relax. You've said you can't discuss your work with me and I'm not going to ask. There is, however, something I want to tell you."

"Oh, God—do we need wine?"

"No, I don't have any wine, but I have got some Diet Cola if you'd like one of those instead."

Nodding, I sit in the lounge while Mum potters about in the kitchen, which is when I realise how bare everything looks. A knot forms in the pit of my stomach.

"You're moving out?" I exclaim as Mum reappears with our drinks.

"I am, indeed. You're paving a way forward in life, and it's about time I did too. I'm moving up to Scotland."

"Scotland!"

"Aye, where they have snow and wee drams, haggis and tartan."

"But…it's so far away."

"Oh, please! It's not like I'm crossing the Atlantic. You can always hop on a plane to come and visit me."

I promptly burst into tears just as the pizza arrives.

~ *Chapter 40* ~

Happy New Year and not so happy birthday to me!

Well, at least it would be *happy* new year if I hadn't been promptly throwing up for most of this morning. God knows how I am going to dance this evening—my legs feel like jelly and my head feels as if it's been repeatedly hit with a heavy wooden mallet. I'm even too sick to feel fearful of what missing tonight's performance will mean for Pink Club.

Christmas had been a low-key affair with Mum having moved away. I had a quiet one over at Sarah and Dante's, eating Christmas lunch and the proverbial crackers and watching cheesy Christmas films. To be quite honest, I'm glad it was over in a blur.

I dry heave in the bathroom for what I hope is one final time, deciding now's a good a time to let Eva know her star of the show will be a no-show.

On picking up my phone, I can already see that Eva has beaten me to the punch. Relief washes over me as I see in her message that she, herself, is unwell and there are a few other members of staff who have become sick with suspected food poisoning.

Bing bong!

My doorbell calmly alerts me to someone's presence.

"Who is it?" I call feebly.

"Hello, Darla? I am Doctor Amelia Khan. I am an in-house doctor for Pink Club."

Oh, thank God for that, I think. "Just a minute!" I call out while pulling the chain and locks off the door with my shaking hands.

"Hello…good morning, or—by the looks of you—perhaps not such a good morning? Right, let's have a look at you. I've been up to my eyeballs in food poisoning cases all morning and I'm pretty sure this is what ails you, but I will double check everything," Doctor Khan says in her rich Indian accent.

Binks jogs to his cat tower to view proceedings at a safe distance, as a stranger has now entered our home. I feel, at times, I should have a sign that says **Beware of Cat**.

"I'm meant to be dancing tonight for a big show. What are my chances of getting any better before this evening?"

"I can give you some anti-nausea medication, but it's better to let these things run their course. You're quite dehydrated and have high key tones and protein in your urine, indicating as such."

"I guess the good Fortune Cookie restaurant where we all ate Chinese at was not so lucky."

"On the contrary, if you were to get sick with food poisoning, better to get it mild like this."

"This is *mild?*" I exclaim.

"You're lucky, as everyone who ate there last night is. You could have been in the hospital."

"I think I'm going to be sick."

"Here—put some of your stomach contents into this tube. Is it just vomiting you've had today?"

By the time Doctor Khan has left, I have been poked, prodded and checked over thoroughly. I was given a small IV bag of fluids that have helped to prop up my hydration and I'm told to expect a follow up appointment the next day.

My mobile rings and I can see that it's Eva. Sighing, and wanting nothing more than to crawl under my bed to go to sleep, I begrudgingly accept the call.

"Hi, Darla. How are you feeling?"

I respond with, "I've been better. I don't think I can eat prawns ever again after this, though."

"Please don't mention prawns to me. I've not since long been for the umpteenth visit to the bathroom myself. Did Doctor Khan come to check up on you?"

"Yes, and she will again tomorrow. I guess this means no big dancing debut tonight then. I would have called you anyway to say I'm not fit to be on that stage – "

"Would you be ok to dance if it wasn't raised up high?"

"I don't actually know." *Oh, God—she can't honestly be expecting me to dance tonight, can she?!!*

"Well, come into the dance studio and see how you feel. I'll be there, as will Octavia. We all got the same food poisoning, so we can suffer together."

Not being funny, but I thought our first team building exercise would involve something more along the lines of paint balling or bowling, not soldiering through not trying to chunder everywhere and over everyone.

"Sure...but first I need sleep."

"Great! See you tonight. I'll send Max to pick you up at 8:30."

I can't wait to say goodbye over the phone, as I'm off bonding with Bob the toilet again. Seeing as we're spending so much time together recently, I decided to name my thoroughly punished porcelain toilet.

The next time I'm aware of anything, having crawled back under my covers, is when Binks is batting at my face with his little grey paws and meowing at me for food. My head is pounding as I sit up gingerly. There is no time for anymore rest, though. I notice that there are now only ninety minutes for me to get my act together.

The nausea has abated, and I actually feel a tad hungry, which is a blessing. Getting up, I wobble over to the kitchen and feed Binks first before putting the oven on to make myself some boiled chicken and rice. An old college friend of mine once told me the best way to beat dehydration was with army grade jungle juice: one pint of water with a teaspoon of sugar and half teaspoon of salt. Gross, but did the job.

Soon I am showered, dressed in my pre–dance clothes, dosed up on paracetamol for my headache, and ready to forge ahead with my best dance performance to date. It was a fast routine and not as intricate or long as the choreography. We had been practicing for the spring gala, but this was my first really big dance performance as an adult in front of a high-class audience. In a way, the food poisoning seems to have rid me of any pre–performance jitters. Now my goal seemed to be just to get to Pink Club and survive the night sick-free.

Max arrived earlier than expected, so I let him in just as I was finishing my supper.

"Hi, Darla. Are you nearly ready to go?"

Jeez, rush much? "Ready whenever you are."

"Sorry to usher you out of the door so fast." Max looks stressed.

As the fresh air hits me, fresh goosebumps break out all over my skin. "Gosh, it's a bit brass monkey, isn't it?"

Max doesn't really acknowledge my comment but instead forges ahead towards the underground car park. We arrive at Pink Club just as the heavens open, so I am very thankful to be able to get out of the car underground. Max comes to open my side of the door and it is then I notice the sound of rotor blades above.

"Royalty must be here early," is all that Max says, leaving my mouth agape as he strides forward to call the lift.

"I've been tasked to stay glued to you for tonight. I am sorry if that might seem a bit awkward."

"No, I'm perfectly ok with that decision." Who am I kidding? I still feel sick and could throw up any minute. Thank God it's not been coming out of both ends. Then I may be having to resign on ground of absolute mortification.

We arrive and Max escorts me to my dressing room. I had been barred from coming in here until Eva could redecorate it. I'm hoping to see her at least at some point this evening before my dancing debut.

The room is an expansive white space. A large silver mirror hangs on one of the walls above a pale pink chaise lounge pitted with bright diamanté buttons. Big swathes of chiffon pink material hang from the ceiling to create a sort of barrier to break up the space. The biggest dressing table I've ever seen stands proudly on the far wall opposite the doorway. Gentle music plays out of an overhead speaker.

Soon, there is a knock on the door, and as I open it, a flurry of people flock inside.

"Hello, my name is Madeleine. I'm your hair and make-up artist this evening. This is Pablo, your costume fitter; Gregory, your masseuse; and Beatrice will be attending to any food or drinks orders you have and any gifts such as flowers and such."

"Gosh, this is all very new to me." *Bloody hell! I've got my own small army of staff! Stick that up your pipe and smoke it, Marie Adams!*

"We're a bit stretched for time and Octavia wants to make sure you have enough of it to run through your performance before you get on stage, so let's get busy and make you B–E–A–U–T–I–F–U–L!" Madeleine exclaims, sitting me down in front of my new dressing table and getting to work straight away.

Within moments, I have Madeleine and Pablo's hands pulling and pinching at me with hair styles and costume adjustments. I bite my tongue every time Pablo seems to accidentally stick me with a pin or Madeleine seems to find a knot in my hair and just wrenches at it with her big bristle brush.

Once my costume has been sized up, Pablo whips it off me, leaving me in my undies, and gets to work fast at a little pop-up station he's created with table and sewing machine.

Gregory then directs me to a massage table where he is pounding and whipping me, informing me of the specified hand movements he is using. My stomach is yelling to me from the inside of how excruciatingly painful everything feels, and I just pray to God it's over soon. Thankfully, the massage ends on a much more relaxed footing before Pablo and Gregory are ushered out of my dressing room by Madeleine, and Beatrice is given an order to get me a power smoothie that is easily digestible. I'm instructed to stay lying on the massage couch, and what happened next I'm pretty sure the whole of London knows about. Madeleine unceremoniously informs me that I need a Brazilian. *Quick* is definitely not less painful. I'll probably be dancing like John Wayne for the rest of the night.

Before I know it, I'm in costume, hair and makeup done, power smoothie down [which was chocolate and indeed very yummy] and being rushed right up to rehearsals. So those guests do not get a glimpse of me, I'm taken through back corridors and get to the next floor on a service lift. Feeling very disorientated now, as we have entered an area of Pink Club I'm not familiar with at all, I hot foot it to keep up with Madeleine, as the last thing anyone needs tonight is for me to get lost again.

~ *Chapter 41* ~

Entering the dance studio, I'm relieved to see that the atmosphere is calm. Octavia is quietly putting the guys through their paces, and it is only then I am aware that no music is playing.

"There she is: the star of the show," Octavia announces, beaming at me, which elicits smiles from Midnight and company who all still look slightly green around the gills.

Silently, we run through our choreography. I'm a bit shaky on the silk rope, and there's an in-depth discussion as to whether we should use them tonight or not. Midnight suggests more simple poses on the rope, and we all nod in agreement.

"Ok guys, if you don't need me now, I think I'll head home," Octavia says as we wrap up our rehearsals.

"Oh…you're not going to watch the show?" My voice doesn't hide my hurt.

"It's actually protocol for security reasons; I'm not a guest, so I don't get the luxury to sit in on the action."

"Oh…well, that's pants."

"Yeah, especially as Madge is a guest tonight and I'm a ma-hoosive fan."

"Wait...*the* Madge is here?"

"The very same. Right, guys, great rehearsal tonight. Look after our girl up there."

"We will protect her with our lives," Digit assures her.

Before Octavia departs, I learn the dance mantra pre-performance, and we all enter our hands into a circle while we pray together. I'm not religious, but it does somehow reinforce the good feeling I have to be united in such a strong dance team.

"Knock, knock," a woman's voice calls. I'm happy to see it's Eva. She walks with me and the gang down to the underground back staging area before pulling me to one side out of sight of Midnight and the others.

"Listen, I don't have much time to explain, but Joshua has requested you wear this necklace of Mimi's for good luck." Eva holds up a pair of golden ballet slippers that dangle from a thin golden chain.

I have lost all use of my voice box, it appears, as Eva affixes the chain around my neck. *Joshua has requested I wear this...why?* I don't have time to ponder on this grand gesture before Midnight ushers me forward to take up my place on the stage. Eva says she will be cheering from the eaves and tells me to break a leg.

Digit, Mixer, Medley and Siren take up their respective places on the pink and black stage. Tonight the stage's internal lights are switched on and it casts an eerie pink glow in the dark space.

Midnight takes my hand as I step up and make my way to stand with him close to the centre.

"Are you sure you're ok to go up high? It's not too late to change your mind," Midnight whispers into my ear, which makes me feel all the tingles.

"I'll be fine; tummy all good now," I assure him, gently patting my stomach.

"Right, then time to get our masks on and bring back the life to this stage with a pink punch," Midnight says, giving me a little fist bump.

We all have been instructed to wear masks for tonight's performance to hide my appearance, as rumours have surfaced that I'm the waitress involved in the 'incident' at Chef No. 9.

Oh, how rude of me—I haven't yet described my costume for you. I am wearing a very short fitted pink dress with a sweetheart top line, no straps, and a fluffy pink Tinker Bell style skirt over the dress. Pale pink shoes sit on my feet, which have been designed to look like glass shoes. My hair has been pulled up into a period drama-style up-do with curls and trestles of hair hanging around my face. Madeleine sprayed non-permanent fuchsia pink spray into my hair to add, yet more, pink tone to my ensemble. My makeup was applied with professional face paint in the design of a butterfly to help hide my features further in case my mask [also a butterfly] slips or falls off.

So, here we are all, present and ready to kick start the new year with a bang, when all of a sudden—*oh no…no, no, no! Not now!* My abdomen clenches and pain rips through my stomach as a sudden attack of IBS hits me like a freight train.

"Sorry, I got to –" I don't even have time to say anything else as I dive off the stage and head for the nearest bathroom, clenching and squeezing as I go and praying to the powers that be that I don't have a fecal incident inside of my pretty pink costume.

My shoes are slowing me down, so I ditch them in a corridor somewhere. I'm now blindly running, desperately seeking out a porcelain friend. Eventually, I find a bathroom and dive straight into it. Thankfully, it's empty, as I imagine all staff must be otherwise occupied, waiting for me to bring the shine back to Pink Club after Bella's death. But Darla would be a no-show, as Darla would now be exploding *off* stage. If anything were to cement my belief there is no God, it is this very situation.

Unbeknown to me, there was now blind panic from everyone as they scramble around trying to find me until Max was able to locate my trajectory to this very bathroom. Once my bowels are thoroughly emptied and I'm feeling hundreds of times better, I realise there is a horrific smell now emanating from the cubicle, and I wish more than ever that I had some of that nice smelly VIP stuff.

Quickly leaving the safety of the cubicle—now well and truly sullied with the pong I left behind—and having washed my hands, I check the bathroom door and am thankful to see there is a lock on it. Someone turns the handle, and without thinking, I lock the door. I have to get rid of the smell; I'll die of embarrassment if I don't. I take the hand soap and tip some down the toilet before flushing, and thankfully it does take some of the smell away.

The door is all but being broken down at this point with shouts from both Max and Eva. I finally unlock the door and open it just as Max is running towards it. He barges through the doorway, smashing into me, and his momentum carries us both forward whereby he slips on some soap I accidentally messed on the floor, which doesn't help to slow us down. I bang my head on the back of one of the sinks, and stars explode all around my vision before momentarily knocking me out.

"Darla…Darla…can you hear me? Darla…she's coming round. Get the first aid kit!" a voice, that sounds far away, yells.

"Who is Darla…no, wait, who am I? *Where* am I? Holy crap—I don't know who I am!" My memory seems to have momentarily evaded me and panic rises within. Then, as swiftly as my memory left the building, it starts to come back to me.

"Ok, so you know who you are now?" Max looks at me, very concerned. His forehead also took a hit on the edge of the sink, and he has a great big egg there now.

"Y–yes…oh my God, the show!"

"Don't worry about it; I've sorted it with the lads and we've got the other entertainers in the ballroom," Eva tells me somberly.

"What happened? Was it stage fright?" Eva asks as Max continues his first aid checks on me.

"I don't know what came over me." *Liar.* "One minute I was fine, the next…well, I was running."

"There is only one thing for it. You have to get up on that stage and dance like you've never danced before," Eva commands, completely ignoring the fact I've just suffered a mild concussion.

"I don't think that's wise," Max interjects.

"With all due respect, Max, this isn't your decision. Do you feel like you can dance, Darla?"

"Yes, I can do it." What the hell am I saying? I just lost my memory! Perhaps it knocked some sense into me. Must remember to keep VIP in my bag at all times after this. See? I can make forward thinking mental memos—I'll be fine.

"I really think Darla needs to be looked at more thoroughly at hospital," Max tells Eva sternly.

"Ok, let's compromise. I will dance, and Max can take me to hospital straight away afterwards."

"I can't force you not to dance; it has to be *your* decision."

"Come on, let's get you back to the stage," Eva suggests, helping me to my feet with Max.

Once steady on my feet, I'm handed my shoes and helped back to the stage where a very pissed-off Midnight and others are found.

"Stage fright, my ass. Next time you're not well enough to dance, don't bother showing up," Midnight growls as he hauls me firmly onto the stage ready to take up our positions.

"FYI, I had a toilet emergency—a *spontaneous* toilet emergency as in *IBS*!" I growl before I can stop myself, and my cheeks redden immediately from sheer embarrassment. I can't see the guy's faces in the dark, lit up only from the glow of the stage lights, but the silence rings loudly in my ears.

"Just don't shit on me!" Siren yells, and we all burst out laughing as the stage rises.

We manage to compose ourselves just moments before we enter the ballroom, which has been sent into darkness as the audience prepares to watch us perform.

~ *Chapter 42* ~

A silence descends upon us, and the space before music and pyrotechnics bring the stage and surrounding area to life.

The room is crammed with people, yet I can't make out any faces, as I'm too busy concentrating on my steps and balancing. My first leap to the silk rope goes really well and I manage to do all of my practiced poses without a hitch. My leap back to the stage has a bit of a wobble, but Midnight expertly manages to conceal this as he helps me back onto the platform, my heart now in my mouth.

Once we finish the routine, feet stomps and clapping with shots of 'Encore' and 'mask off' can be heard, but to keep interest piqued, we are only allowed the one performance before we descend back into the depths of the basement backstage area.

Eva and a group of other back staging staff are there ready to congratulate me and the dance safety team. Eva pops a cork off a bottle of pink champagne and flutes are rapidly handed out by bar staff. Midnight lifts me onto his shoulders as we proceed en-masse to a brighter space where everyone starts singing, "For she's a jolly good fellow."

I don't have long with everyone before Max is ready to take me to hospital, as it was agreed I would do just that. I honour my word to him and reluctantly leave the celebrations to first change out of my costume back in my dressing room where there is an array of floral gifts, teddy bears and quite as few boxes of luxury chocolates.

Eva joins me and hands me a flute of pink champagne which I swiftly drink up. She has already arranged my gifts to be delivered to my apartment, but I ask her to deliver a huge bunch of blue and white flowers to Dante and Sarah's apartment along with one of the teddy bears and boxes of chocolate for them to share and a bottle of the pink champagne [that I was now missing out on]. I also ask her to give the rest of my gifts to the staff, including herself, because it's only thanks to everyone that tonight went off without a hitch.

"Good luck at the hospital. Let me know as soon as you know anything," Eva says, giving me a hug.

Then Max knocks on the door, asking if I'm ready to go.

Once in the car, I'm amazed how fast everything happened. I was also gutted that I didn't get to meet Madge or any of the other celebrities and high-profile guests. Eva has assured me, though, that come the spring gala, I will have time to meet everyone on a more personal level, as my identity would then be revealed.

"There is a small gift for you in the small panel under your seat. It's from Joshua, who says happy birthday, by the way."

I reach down and manage to open the concealed compartment under my seat. I find a neat little box wrapped in silver paper, tied with a pink bow. My heart thunders away excitedly as I gingerly open my birthday present. Inside is a framed Polaroid photograph of me on stage dancing. It's such a beautiful shot and I find the sentiment truly touching. The frame is glass so you can see the front and back of the photo. On the back is a message that reads:

"Congratulations on your first big performance with us here at Pink Club. Happy Birthday and New Year!" ~Joshua Glass

I feel the blood flood to my face as I hold the small, but no less thoughtful, gift in my hands.

Dante then calls me, and I pause before answering, as it suddenly dawns on me that I haven't thought of my crush on him for a while now. I must be over him.

"Oh, hey, D. How did tonight go? We were both thinking of you."

"It went really well, thanks. I didn't get to mingle since this was just a taster session for the guests, but it was good."

"See? I knew you were born to do this; you're a natural—how could they not love you. Hey, listen, Sarah and I…we have some news. When is your next day off?"

"I'm not sure; let me just have a look." Muting Dante, I press the speaker button so Max can hear me.

"You don't happen to know if I'm needed back here tomorrow, do you?"

"There is no instruction for me to arrange you to be brought back tomorrow. I can help you pull a sicky if you like. I regularly had to do this with Bella, but you have a genuine reason," Max responds, pointing to his head.

"That would be great if you could. Thanks, Max."

"No worries, and Mum's the word, ok?" he says, winking at me through the rearview mirror.

Taking the phone off mute, I confirm with Dante that I can see them tomorrow.

~ *Chapter 43* ~

The hospital gives me a clean bill of health but tells me I am to be monitored overnight at home. Seeing as I have no one to offer to help with this, Max tells me he will sleep in the guest bedroom, and I know it's not a request. It doesn't feel awkward—he has only ever been the professional bodyguard/security guard—and I'm beginning to think of him less like a human and more like that Rottweiler guard dog they have back at Pink Club.

Eva has left me an excited voicemail to tell me I was a big hit with everyone, and they can't wait to see me perform at the spring gala. She also tells me to take the rest of the week off, which means no sicky pulled from me, which make me feel lighter.

I run myself a bath, leaving the TV on a news channel that is talking about the New Year's Eve events.

Washing away the any remnants of last year, I leave the bathroom feeling clean and refreshed. I call my mother to wish her a Happy New Year and we end up doing a video chat, sharing a glass of bubbly before I sign off.

Fatigue fully sets in now that the adrenaline is well and truly wearing off. Climbing into bed with my favourite sushi pyjamas on, I'm asleep within mere moments, Binks asleep at the foot of my bed.

* * * * *

"Darla! Darla! Wake up!" I hear Max yelling while trying to break my door down.

"Whatever is the matter?!" I yell, now fully awake.

"The apartment building is on fire! We have to leave—NOW!"

"Shit! *Shit, shit, shit!*" Jumping out of bed and grabbing Binks, I wrench my bedroom door open and begin to fall down a great big black gaping hole.

"*AHHHHHHHHHHHHHHHHHHHHHHHHHH!*" I scream as I fall. I squeeze my eyes tight while waiting to hit the ground.

Hands grab me just before I meet my maker, and—while thrashing around, disorientated by the darkness—it takes me a moment to realise that I am, in fact, still in my bedroom. Max is gently holding my shoulders, having woken me up. My bedroom door is completely off its hinges and lying in a heap on the floor.

"Are you ok? You seemed to be having a nightmare. Sorry about the door—force of habit. I'll get someone round to fix it tomorrow," Max says as his mobile phone rings.

"Sir…yes, she is fine…bad dream…very well; I shall be there shortly."

"Who was that?"

"Mr. Glass requires me to drive him to the airport. There's a family emergency. Will you be ok on your own?"

"I feel fine; bit shaken from the nightmare, but I'm ok," I reply, secretly crestfallen that Max must leave so soon, as the residual feelings of the nightmare still linger for me.

Lying in bed with a now great big gaping hole where my bedroom door used to reside, I decide there's nothing for it. I will have to get up. Binks must have shot off my bed from all the commotion, as I can't see him.

Max has made me a coffee with my new coffee maker in my new fancy kitchen. Will I ever get used to this lifestyle? It might grow on me, but I've never been someone to live beyond their means.

"Right, you're sure you'll be ok?" Max asks while putting his suit jacket on.

"Yes, I think I'd have to be pretty unlucky to have an apartment fire the same day I dreamt of one."

"A guy called Adam will be here at some point today to fix your door. Sorry again for that." Max ignores my comment about the dream. He seems a bit on edge—distracted somehow—but then again, he's needed in two places at once, so can't say I'm surprised.

Once he has left, I see Binks, so I get him some food and decide on having a lazy day at home until meeting Dante and Sarah later. I settle onto the sofa with my coffee in the lounge and switch on my massive TV. I am not prepared for what's about to flash up on the news headlines.

Mimi Glass is ALIVE!

She's currently being treated in a high-end London hospital. The details are sketchy, but it looks like her body was mis-identified and she has, in fact, been held as a captive for the last five years! I watch the news reporter's lips moving while speaking, but little else is registering with me as I realise how significant this will be for Joshua and his parents. And Pink Club! I burst into tears as my hand automatically goes to the golden ballet slipper pendant now hanging around my neck.

She's alive! All this time…alive!

To Be Continued…

Printed in Great Britain
by Amazon